THE NOMAD

The Nomad

Justin Sexton

Above the Rain Collective

2024

Above the Rain Collective
abovetheraincollective@gmail.com
North Georgia, USA

Contributing Editor: J.A. Sexton

Publisher's note:

This is a work of fiction. All characters and incidents are the product of the author's imagination, places are used fictitiously and any resemblance to an actual person, living or dead, is entirely coincidental.

ISBN: 979-8-9899186-0-7

Cover graphics and interior formatting by J.A. Sexton
Above the Rain logo artwork by Bee Freitag
Cover art: Justin Sexton

TO PHOENIX

PROLOGUE

A murder of crows echoed through the holler. As they fluttered overhead, the professor couldn't believe his eyes. He lifted the solid oak chest out of the dark, hollow earth with both hands and carefully placed it on the ground at their feet.

His assistant and a fellow archaeologist watched as he tenderly cleaned the wooden box off. It had intricate gold trim and the entire piece was a deep, earthy umber. Even after almost a hundred and fifty years underground, the treasure chest still looked like a beautiful work of art.

They all huddled together as the professor opened the box. They each took a deep breath; they'd worked tirelessly together over the last seven years in search of the relic they now loomed over. The clasp of the chest snapped open, revealing the treasure inside.

"I don't believe it! It's the skull, perfectly intact!" Noah exclaimed.

All three eye sockets were clearly visible as the skull sat appearing dull and muted against the glorious backdrop of Crow's gold.

"Tell me that wasn't a message from the heavens, a murder of crows flies above us the moment we find Crow and Coyote's treasure. I don't know what else to say, y'all. Thank you," the professor expressed as tears of joy slid down his face.

His entire life led to this moment. Ever since he was a little boy, Noah knew he wanted to be an archaeologist. He grew up in the Appalachian mountains. His family was from Ireland and Scotland, then migrated to America in the very late eighteen hundreds.

They eventually settled in southern Appalachia; in Georgia and Tennessee. His family history was full of folklore and mythology. His grandfather, a historian, always told him tales of mythical creatures and cosmic entities.

The Appalachian mountains contained a very rich history of ancient folklore and the professor consumed all of those stories like candy as a child. To him, they were more than just epic fables of fictional beings, rather chronicles of the creation of Earth, its people, animals, time, and space. His favorite, however, was the Legend of the Nomad.

Noah and his crew spent several years searching for evidence that proved the validity of the story. Now, they had that proof. He closed the chest and they began working on bringing it safely back to the university. Winter break was coming to an end and he'd be back to teaching in a week. He couldn't wait to tell his students.

He was certain they wouldn't believe him.

After all, who would?

"To think, only a few years ago, we confirmed the first cave drawing," he said to his assistant as he wiped the tears from his face.

~

Seven years prior, during the summer of 1993, Noah and his team spent several weeks in the craggy mountains of Maine, trying to locate a cave drawing of the Nomad. A few hikers had taken pictures of it after discovering the image during spring break. One of the hikers emailed the photographs to Noah and he took the chance in early June to make the trek to find the illustration and validate its legitimacy. He located the cave in Maine and saw the drawing. Confirming its authenticity was the first real stepping stone in the team's journey.

After that, the pieces came together. They confirmed another identical petroglyph in the North Georgia mountains a few years later, and one in the highlands of Scotland earlier the past summer. All three glyphs were found in caves and they all appeared to be identical. There was no variation in how they were drawn. The detail in the erratic line work was consistent across the board. However, they certainly seemed to be hand-painted and dated over five hundred million years old.

The unearthing of the treasure and the three-eyed skull was the final piece in an ancient puzzle. Not only did the gold confirm Crow and Coyote's story, the skull proved the existence of the legendary Moss People, which in turn would open the floodgates of folklore and ancient mythology.

Noah and his team brought the relic to the University of Appalachia where he was head of the Archaeology

Department. There it would undergo extensive tests and research to confirm its age. The professor knew with all his heart this was the real deal. Ever since he was a little boy, he knew this day would come. He was so obsessed with the tale of the Nomad growing up, his friends called him Noah the Nomad.

Winter break ended and everyone returned to school. Noah couldn't wait to tell his students about their discovery. His first lecture that morning was his nine a.m. Mythology and Folklore class. He entered the university building feeling elated. Students shouted back and forth while they took their seats. He entered the auditorium as butterflies filled his belly.

"Greetings, class. I hope everyone had a nice holiday. Happy New Year. I see we all survived Y2K." The class snickered as the professor continued.

"Welcome to Folklore and Mythology. I am your teacher Dr. Noah Greene. Today is a day I've waited my whole life for. As many of you know, I spent the holiday break hunkered down in the deep ravines of the mountainous terrain of our beautiful landscapes here in North Georgia. My team and I have been working hard for seven years, trying to find the infamous Crow's Gold. Today, I'm ecstatic to say we've found it and it's here at the university. It will be undergoing various tests and carbon dating to determine its age, as well as any data we can gather from the skull that was in the chest with the gold."

The class began to cheer and applaud their teacher.

"Thank you. This is a huge step in learning humanity's true origins. Ever since I was a little boy, I've been fascinated by the awe and wonder of the Appalachian mountains. Nothing on this planet is older than this great mountain range around us. There is endless knowledge of mystery and lore that radiates from the shaping and formation of this great chain. The hills here are much like mankind. The more worn down you are by time, the wiser you are. The mountains of Appalachia know no boundaries for they are the gateway to our beginning. Before Pangea, they ran all the way above the ocean to Scotland; they were known as the Central Pangean Mountains.

Eventually, they split up, becoming the Scottish Highlands, the Atlas, and the Appalachian mountain ranges. They were massive and much bigger than they are today; more comparable to the Himalayas, which are just babies in comparison of age. By the beginning of the Permian period, around two hundred and ninety million years ago, the Central Pangean range was at its peak elevation.

During that era, the terrain was subjected to extreme weathering, reducing the mountain peaks to around half their original size. This created numerous deep valleys. By the Triassic era, they were severely reduced in size yet again. Then, about two hundred million years ago, the Pangean range in Western Europe shrank to a few hilly areas surrounded by deep ocean basins.

Flash forward to today, and we have what we're all familiar with. In this class this semester, we'll focus in-depth on Appalachian and Native folklore and how it ties to Celtic mythology. When the Pangean mountains were formed, so much energy and focus came to be during that moment. From that rise, came the birth of beings, creatures, and gods who are reflected in these ancient legends and depictions. When the tectonic plates shifted and Pangea was abandoned, the Appalachian mountains were born, and from that birthing emerged the Nomad.

To fully comprehend the magnitude of the discovery of not only Crow's Gold, but also the proof that a race of visionary people with three eyes existed, and possibly do still exist today, you must understand the true legend of the Nomad and his role in the discovery of this great treasure. Class, sit back, relax, and buckle up. This is the legend of the Nomad."

CHAPTER ONE

"Drop the ax," the man growled.

"Drop the pistol," Crow replied, gripping the wooden handle firmly in her grasp.

"Where's my brother Ellis?"

"I don't know where the son of bitch is, last I remember, he was begging for his life," Crow said through her teeth, clenching her nails further into the light wood grain.

"Drop the hatchet or I *will* shoot. Your time is up, the race is over," the old man proclaimed.

"Tell me where my brother is and I'll give it back, all the gold," Crow answered.

"Last I saw him, his skinny ass was dying at the top of the mountain. Right where I left him!" the man hollered as he made his way closer to Crow, pistol pointed at her throat.

"I don't believe you! We had a deal and I have everything you want. All of it!" she shouted as she raised the ax higher in the air.

Crow had a reputation for being aggressive and deadly with the blade. She'd killed her fair share of men. Times were rough and she and her brother had done everything they could to survive harsh times.

"I don't know what to tell you, he's dead."

"Then we don't have a deal," she spat as she charged toward the man.

He went to pull the trigger but it didn't fire. Confused and afraid, the man tried once again to shoot at Crow, but the gun wouldn't budge. He watched as a murder of crows emerged from her back in the shape of crescent wings and put him in a hallucinogenic trance. The crows sat in perfect unison, forming carefully crafted wings that extended majestically out from her shoulder blades.

It didn't always happen, it wasn't something mechanical she could control. She never understood it. After her family and village were slain, she'd have bouts of magic. As the black wings spread out and each crow held its place firmly, her eyes turned gray. As quickly as she could, she swung the ax at the man, knocking him clear in the face and to the ground below. The blood began to pool around the man's body and seep into the pearl-white snow, covering the frozen earth beneath her feet. His body seized and convulsed in the snow, twitching and shrieking through the evening ether.

The crows each flew off into the night air, only to return seconds later with gold trinkets in their talons. She collected her riches and spit on the dead man's face, slipping the gold pieces into her satchel as the crows began to feast on the scoundrel's flesh. Her saliva dripped off his gray beard as the blood seeped out. There was a time when she'd felt sadness when she killed someone but times had become so rigid, she no longer felt remorse.

After all, every person she'd killed was a vile human being, dead set on destroying everything and everyone around them for gold. Gold was life and its discovery led to an influx of scavengers and savages in search of an easy get-rich fix. The harsh reality was, it wasn't that easy and it cost many their lives. All the accessible gold had been found quickly and most of the prospectors made their way elsewhere. Only lazy degenerates remained. Crow and her brother, Coyote, were not the norm for the mountain gold town. They'd both been fortunate to escape being slaughtered by berserkers who'd ransacked their small, rural, mountainside village.

One morning, they'd been told by their father to set out on a day hunt. Just after they headed out for the morning, the village was brutally attacked. Crow and Coyote were the only survivors. They'd heard the screams from the woods but there was nothing they could do to protect the village with only the two of them.

Crow's mind returned to the current moment and she reached into the man's pants, pulling out a pocket watch. She checked the time before slipping it into her satchel. The watch was pure gold with a crow engraved on it.

"Fitting," she said to herself as she called the murder back to her.

She always collected something from those she killed; a token to remember them by. After all, it was more than what the men had done for her family. They devoured everyone and set everything on fire, only ash remained. There was nothing physical or tangible left, only fleeting memories. Her brother was all she had left. She hoped the man was bluffing; the brothers needed to keep both Crow and Coyote alive in order to get their treasure.

That was the deal.

The man's entire family tracked them for weeks and they'd finally caught up to the siblings. Crow knew she needed to make her way up the mountain fast and find Coyote before he froze to death. Gathering her senses, she started traversing up the mountainside. The incline was rugged and rocky at times, forcing her to climb on her hands and knees. Finally, she reached a pathway and began making headway. The snow was falling harder and the temperature was dropping; Coyote's time was running out. Crow trudged through the snow as fast as she could, slowly making progress.

As it fell, it made the trek even tougher. Her feet were slipping on the road, which was hardly a pathway at all, just a lightly used walkway made by hikers forging their own path. The route was beginning to become less clear and Crow was losing her way, her peripheral blocked by heavy snow precipitation with the wind howling. She paused for a moment and thought of her brother, a memory of them as young children washing over her. She could see the sun hitting the lake as they were fishing with their father early one summer morning.

"Father, why do bad things happen to good people?" Coyote asked, a bright, blue sky full of light transient clouds filling the landscape behind him.

"It's simple, my children. Earth is cruel, and life is unfair. The only thing guaranteed is suffering. Every moment is a lesson," their father replied.

"You didn't answer the question," Coyote said.

"Every moment is a lesson, son. Never forget that. Our people have been here for a very long time, this land is our home and we never take it for granted. It is not ours to take, it does not belong to us, yet it gives its life and its vitality to us each and every day. It is our food, our shelter, our place of community, our storm, our peaks, our valleys. It was here before us and it will be here well after we are all gone. At any moment, Spirit may strip it all from us and that is something we must be ready for at all times."

Crow pulled herself back to the present, her head hung low. She began to feel an emotion swell up that she was unfamiliar with... defeat. Her spirit was broken and undone. She felt as if she had nothing left to give but if she gave up now, it would cost Coyote his life. He was all she had left and without him, she'd be left lost and abandoned. The fear of isolation began to snake its way through her mind. The snow fell harder as the deciduous trees creaked and moaned in the wind. The mixture of orchestrated howls and syncopated squeaks made the wilderness seem even more haunting.

"I can't give up, not now," she whispered to herself, digging her boots into the ice and increasing her speed up the mountainside.

Her hands covered in blisters and her fingers bloody, she pressed on even further up the final climb over the upper outcropping.

"This is where the old man said he left him," she muttered to herself.

She froze for a moment, her heart beating in and out of her chest in perfect synchronization with the swaying of the trees in the breeze. A faint sound in the distance caught her attention.

"Coyote is that you?" she called out.

"Crow..." he replied with the small amount of energy he had left.

"I hear you, I'm coming toward you," she yelled out as she ran swiftly toward her brother. When she got to him, she was furious by the sight. They had beaten him to shit. Every part of him was bloody and bruised. The right side of his face was completely swollen, he was almost unrecognizable. He could barely speak and was clinging to what little life remained in him.

"Coyote, I'm so sorry. We've got to get you down the mountain before you freeze to death," she whispered as tears slowly streamed down her face. She took off her coat and wrapped it around him.

"It's going to be tough, but I'm going to carry you down this mountain. Thank the Spirit you're a skinny fucker," she said as she wrapped her arms around her brother and flipped him over her shoulder.

CHAPTER TWO

C row and Coyote's village was unique to the area. Their people lived minimalisticly and sustainably and for a long time, tucked in the mountainside. They took only what they needed and also thanked the gods for their generous offerings.

The village was newly formed. They'd recently come together with another group of feral mountain folk over the last season in an effort to have more protection against outsiders. Their parents combined with others hidden in the area to create a protective community where they could live more in line with their wild and simple lifestyle.

There'd been a shift in their previous community and their family traveled north back to the sacred land. Everyone had their role based on their knowledge and strengths. Crow and Coyote were just like their father and excelled at hunting and fishing. They did the majority of the hunting between the three of them.

The village was thankfully small, so hunts were planned out twice a week; one early morning hunt and an evening trip if the moon was bright that cycle. Sometimes, they'd light torches along the riverbanks to increase their visibility and to help catch their prey.

During a late-night hunt one summer when they were young, there was a terrible accident. They were stalking deer along the riverside and their father hit a huge buck with his bow. In an effort to trap the deer, Coyote had to maneuver around a boulder nestled on some rocks along the riverbank. The buck managed to ram Coyote with its legs and kicked him into the river.

The water was very aggressive that day after a week of rain, and he got dragged under. His right arm managed to get caught between heavy boulders in the river. He screamed in agony, his face barely above water. He began to sink further as the river fought against him.

Their father used a hunting knife and cut Coyote's arm off from the forearm down before he drowned. He was pulled under for some time and believed he died for a moment before coming back to life. Not only did he lose his arm, he also suffered brain damage from oxygen deprivation. The fine motor skills and mental clarity he once had vanished in an instant.

It was tough for Coyote, taking him some time to begin to accept what happened. He struggled with depression immensely after that. He wasn't as skilled at hunting and he wasn't invited out on as many treks after the accident. He felt useless and diminished. His role in the village changed at that time, but he was still invited on occasional outings.

The night before the morning of the surprise attack, their father was acting strange as if he sensed something. He woke them both up before dawn and told them to head out immediately to hunt. They thought it was odd, especially considering Coyote hadn't been invited recently. They certainly hadn't done a trip just the two of them in a long time. Deep down, they felt their father knew the attack was coming as it happened a mere hour after they set off.

Their father was a very fair and honest man, one every child in the village inspired to be like. Both Crow and Coyote struggled deeply with the loss of their family. Not only had they lost their way of life and the ones they loved, they also lost those who guided them. Their world shrunk down to nothing. All they knew now was a life of two.

A life with only each other.

They'd always been close, but the tragedy brought them closer. They needed to be in order to survive. Any word that two hillside folks were seen in the fields or forests and they were done for. The savages would search for lost nomads, scouring the mountains and hold them captive. They'd torture them, scalp them, or just beat the shit out of them for fun or until they told them where gold was.

The individuals still hanging around the mountains in search of an easy treasure hunt were lost and disconnected. Most were bootleggers, murderers, and thieves. They brought nothing but suffering to the hills and they'd destroyed most of it. There wasn't any gold left, only tiny morsels that required sure luck to find.

Occasionally, a local prospector would find a big nugget or two in the river and then everyone would flock to that location to find whatever they could. Most of the time nothing else was found. All the pathetic drones parading around would leave empty-handed. Sometimes, they'd get drunk on moonshine and go looking for village folk to hunt down, but those, too, were becoming scarce just like the folk.

The villages all lived a simple life strategically, something the outsiders never understood. They lived in small, communal areas hidden in the mountainsides and used every bit of the animals they hunted. They didn't use guns, only spears, bows, axes, hatchets, and knives. Those were enough to survive until the outsiders came.

In just a few years, the outsiders destroyed mountains, caves, and forests. They murdered thousands just for an earthly element. Crow and Coyote tried to stay optimistic and live their life in their village's honor, but they were beginning to feel cursed.

That was until their luck changed one rainy night. The weather shifted that evening from sunny and clear to heavy rain and thunderstorms. The rivers were filling up fast and rising. Crow and Coyote were out hunting and foraging quietly. They'd ventured further out than usual and found themselves on a mountainside they weren't familiar with.

When the weather shifted from beautiful to harsh, they decided to look for a safe place to hunker down until the rain stopped. They made their way toward the base of a mountain where they could hear the faint sounds of two men arguing.

"Do you hear that?" Crow asked.

"Yeah, someone's close by. They're loud as hell, though, if we can hear them over this rain and thunder."

"No kidding, they sound pissed. If we're really quiet, we can get closer. There's no way they'll hear us over the storm and themselves yelling. Follow me," Crow whispered as she crouched through the saturated trees and slowly made her way near the men.

As they got close, they saw the two men were digging intensely. The siblings could tell by their conversation, the men were disagreeing about where to bury what they were hiding.

"Right here, it's the most obvious spot, you prick," the tall, bearded fellow said to the shorter gentlemen.

"Fine, I'm soaked and need a drink. Bury this shit and let's go."

The men dug as fast as they could. They weren't digging a grave by the size of it, unless it was for an animal or small person. The men stood there a bit longer, placing rocks over the top of it. Once they were done, they vanished off into the rain. Crow and Coyote waited until the men were gone for some time, then went to dig up what they'd buried.

"Start hitting the ground with your hatchet, Coyote. We'll get whatever this is dug up fast," she said as she started hacking the ground with her ax. It didn't take long for them to find it.

"I hit something," Coyote stated as he reached into the dark, umber earth and retrieved the vessel. He pulled out a three-foot by three-foot chest and lifted it out of the ground. It was as dark as the deep brown earth saturated below. The chest was full oak and had gold trim along the seams.

"Coyote, you open it up, look inside, and tell me what it is. I hope it's gold."

"It's gold, it's fucking gold," he replied in amazement.

"How much?"

"It's hard to tell, but it's pretty full,"

"No wonder it was so heavy," Crow said.

"What the hell? There's a skull in here, too?"

"Let me see." Crow peered inside the chest to see a worn human skull with three eye sockets surrounded by gold.

"What do we do?"

"We keep it, we gotta get it out of here, though, and fast in case those men come back."

"The skull, too?" Coyote asked.

"Yeah, we can use the skull to our advantage in the future."

"Ok, the trunk is heavy, what should we do?"

"I say we drag it a thousand feet, or so, that way. Wait till morning. Hopefully, the rain lets up and we can gather a bunch to take with us, then hide the rest to come back for," Crow replied.

"Alright, let's do it! Let's take what we can now and bury the rest with the head."

"Works for me. We lucked out tonight."

"Hell yeah, we did. It's about time."

CHAPTER THREE

M orning came and the rain stopped. The siblings gathered what they felt was sufficient and easy to carry, then searched for a safe spot to hide the rest.

"We're going to have to bury it, it's the only option," Crow suggested.

"You're right, but we need to find a spot we'll recognize and certainly remember when we come back. We don't know this area, so it may be tricky," Coyote replied as his eyes peered at the endless trees before them.

"What about under that oak tree, right over there? The one that looks like a hand. Look, it even has five fingers." Crow pointed to a tree with just a few leaves left hanging on the branches from late autumn.

"It's the most distinctive one out here. The rest all look the same and we need to do this now, so it works for me."

"Sounds good, let's start digging, and go deeper than those fools did," Coyote urged.

They dug for a bit and developed a nice pit. They lifted the chest into the hole and began filling it in, ensuring they packed the soil down as much as they could.

"That's good, we're far enough out, this should work for now. We can come back in a week after we stash this bit near camp," Crow mentioned as she put her foot on the ground and pushed it down one last time for security.

"Take a mental note, Crow."

"I am, let's head out and come back soon."

They headed out for the week and made the long trek back to their camp. When they got back to their site, they found it'd been ransacked and debris was everywhere.

"Shit, someone was here! We gotta pack up and get out now, back on the move. Let's head west for a few days, then loop back around the mountain toward the gold."

"Ok. Fuck, Crow, this is getting tiresome. We can't seem to catch a break. It's endless, they're going to win. They'll catch us and when they do, they'll torture us."

"They won't catch us, we're smart and quiet on our feet. We have to get back to sleeping in shifts at night, though, to stay alert," Crow muttered.

"Yeah, until the heat dies down."

"We just stole someone's gold, it's never dying down."

"That's true," Coyote said as he laughed and glanced at the sky.

"Spirit's looking out for us, Coyote. We'll get by."

"I hope so, sis."

"Me too," Crow answered faintly.

They gathered what they could and headed out for a few days to hang out in the cliffs and lay low. They found a new spot to camp in the mouth of a cave about fifteen hundred feet up a rocky hill slope. It was tough to access, so they figured they'd be safe there for a few weeks if not months, and could use it as a base and place to hide gold.

"What are we going to do with this gold, Crow? No one will sell anything to us or trade for it. We're even more of a target if we show our hand."

"I don't know, but we'll figure it out. Not all the outsiders are bad, there's got to be a few good seeds out there we can find, hopefully. If we head north, we can trade and buy goods."

"I feel like we're getting by solely on hope," Coyote muttered.

"Sometimes that's all we got."

"It's a dangerous game, a really dangerous game."

"Right now, it's what we got!" Crow repeated.

"Yeah, that's true, it's still a dangerous game," Coyote countered.

"You're right. I don't know what you want me to say, Coyote. This is where we're at," Crow said as she blatantly showed her irritation with the conversation. She was often the optimistic one as Coyote had fallen victim to circumstances and sometimes expected the worst.

"I understand. I love you, Crow."

"I love you too, brother, let's get some rest tonight. Tomorrow we gotta get up early and start camouflaging the mouth of the cave a bit, then set out for firewood and food."

"Good night, shithead."

"Night, Skinny," Crow murmured to him as she drifted off to sleep.

That night, Coyote had a dream, unlike any dream he had before. The entire surrounding forests were covered in a blanket of snow like they'd never seen and the trees were filled with human heads and rotting flesh. In an instant, the scenery shifted and snow owls began appearing as if they were suddenly migrating to the area. They started to fill each branch of every tree as far as Coyote could see. The trees were iridescent at times and shimmered like moonlight in the night sky. They began to sing in an orchestrated display. It sounded like a choir of low-resonating hums that vibrated his entire body. He began to lift into the air and leave Earth, traveling far above the stars up into endless infinity.

Everything around him turned to complete darkness and he saw his father standing there in front of him. "Son, return the treasure before it's too late. Please, I am begging you, it is cursed."

"Father, we're already cursed, how could things get any worse?" Coyote replied.

"You will lose your life, Coyote. Your sister will lose all she has left. Please return the gold and save yourself." His father vanished and the dark space began to grow uncomfortable.

Bodies stacked on top of each other began to rise out from under Coyote's feet. Skulls and bones slowly descended from the tops of the trees, as if they were strung together with fishing line.

He tried to run and scream, but he couldn't move. Something had its hand around his throat, he felt like he was suffocating as he struggled to breathe. When he awoke, he was punching through the cool night air with such vigor, he almost dislocated his left shoulder. His screaming woke up Crow, who was fast asleep.

"Coyote, you ok? You have a bad dream?"

"We need to return the gold tomorrow. I had a dream and saw our father in it. He told me I'd die if we kept it. I don't want to risk it, Crow, it's not worth it."

"Don't be silly, it's just a dream."

"I don't think so, I think you're wrong. We gotta give it back," Coyote demanded.

"We're *not* giving it back. Those men are savages that deserve to die, we can figure out how to get out of here. There's gotta be somewhere safer further north."

"I am washing my hands of this, Crow."

Crow didn't respond. She closed her eyes and pretended to go to sleep. Coyote didn't sleep the rest of the night, he was certain his dream was prophetic. He thought about leaving and going solo, but he knew he wouldn't last long without his sister. After all, he needed her whether he liked it or not. He depended on her to hunt and protect him at times.

Since the accident, Coyote continued to climb down a tunnel of darkness. The boy everyone in the village thought would be their leader one day and follow in his father's footsteps, quickly became a pariah. There was a part of Coyote that was jealous of Crow, but he knew those feelings were only a product of condition. He pushed his feelings aside habitually, they had no place at the surface, especially during times of refuge.

When morning came, they didn't speak to each other. The tension was high and they were falling victim to the chaos consuming them. They ate a breakfast of freshly caught trout and took it easy for the afternoon, mostly gathering firewood and foraging.

"You're looking skinnier than usual, we gotta get a deer hunt in, it's been weeks. We've been getting by fishing and staying quiet, however, we could use the extra meat, bones, and hide," Crow mentioned to Coyote as she split logs with her ax, tossing small lumber against a dead tree stump with a blanket of turkey tail fungi covering it. Coyote didn't respond, he didn't like discussing his weight. It made him feel fragile and delicate, he hated that feeling.

"Are you going to give me the silent treatment today? Whatever, Skinny. I'm tired of looking after you, anyway, do your own hunting," Crow muttered in irritation.

"It's easy for you to say, you got it easy."

"Easy? Neither of us has it easy right now, Coyote. I know it's tough, and I know your situation makes everything worse, but you can't lie around feeling sorry for yourself. We're in the wild. You'll die out here. Get it together for both of us. I love you, I don't want to be alone," she said as she tried to hide her emotion and resumed chopping.

"Maybe I'm feeling sorry for myself. Losing everyone and dealing with vile scum daily. Having to live a life of secrecy, solely because of where you live and who you are is hell, but it does nothing to sit around and mull over the pain. You're right, Crow. But we gotta get out of here, away from the suffering. I can't do it anymore, no matter how much I love this land. It's been stripped of us and its essence. It's time to go elsewhere. I think we should start to travel south toward the ocean."

"That's a long journey, Coyote. I'm honestly not sure it's one you're cut out for, at the moment. We need to go somewhere closer, but more secure for the time being. I think we should head north, far up into the mountains. We're going to need to work together to be safe."

"You only want to trade gold. I don't want to travel further into these mountains. Something is lurking in the hills that's sinister. It's stalking all of us. I can feel it. It's why the evil here continues to grow and flourish. It has something to feed off of. I'm not going further into the mountains. I want to head south," Coyote replied.

"Tough shit. We need to. We need supplies and resources. Plus, we can protect ourselves from that which lurks. It hasn't got us yet. We're protected. As long as I have this amulet and you have yours, we're safe. If we can get up near Signal Mountain, we can trade there."

"These amulets can't protect us forever and you don't know if we can do shit at Signal Mountain. You're going off ancient chatter."

"No, I'm going off knowledge," Crow said with extreme certainty.

"Why, because of folklore?"

"It's not lore if it's your ancestors. The other half of our people went there when the split happened. We can take the gold there to trade and find safety... hopefully."

"There's that word again," Coyote pointed out as he blew on the fire to get it going. He may have lost most of his hunting skills, but he was still resourceful at building a roaring fire.

"Are you in?" Crow asked.

"Fine. You win... again. Yeah, I'm in," he answered in defeat.

"Ok. I say we skip a hunt today. Let's go fish and catch as much as we can. We'll eat good tonight, then tomorrow we head back to the gold and the skull. We'll grab as much as we can carry. It will be heavy but we can do it. I'll carry more, I'll be fine. We should be able to get there in about nine or ten days."

"That's so much to carry, there's no way we'll move at that rate on foot," Coyote suggested.

"Ok, two weeks, then. It will be a couple of days to get up to Cricket's Gap. Maybe once we're there, we can begin getting rid of this gold and start lightening the load," Crow responded as she threw a log on the fire.

They spent the rest of the afternoon fishing and preparing for their journey the next day.

Unfortunately, Mother Nature had other plans.

Chapter Four

H is sister was aware of the aftermath of the accident and how the incident affected her brother mentally and emotionally. Coyote became more reclusive, quiet, and aloof. He talked about his dreams as if they were more concrete than the life he and Crow were living. He spoke about seeing spirits or entities that were not there, as if part of him was still connected to the underworld. Their village had deep beliefs rooted in the spirit realm and its role in the creation of Earth. A lot of those elements and motifs had begun to unfold before Coyote, he was feeling more and more between two worlds as time went on. The dreams to him were peeks into the future... and it was bleak.

Sometimes, he'd forget what lifetime it even was. He'd ramble on about the layers of the universe and the blanket of dark energy permeating all of space. Coyote was buried in it. He knew where he came from, but he had no idea where he was going. Nomadic as they were, both Crow and her brother were caught in an endless cycle they couldn't walk out of. They had to break the pattern. Everything rooted in their ancestry had been devoured; all they had left were their amulets. They'd been given to them by their parents at birth.

Life in the village, though restricted, was not sheltered. They were taught to be aware the world was full of impermanence and nothing was guaranteed. They believed in a collection of entities and shapeshifters making up a greater whole. Coyote always found he gravitated toward the darker spirits, the ones that sought revenge and misfortune on those who were selfish and greedy.

However, he'd learned over time the difference between dark spirits and evil beings. Dark spirits were simply rooted in the earth and in the absence of light, while the evil beings wished harm and sought to destroy everyone and everything in their path.

"There's no way we can head out in this weather, we need to stay safe and dry here in the cave until it lets up," Crow suggested, feeling uneasy about staying in the cave longer.

They'd already been there for a while and normally kept on the go constantly to avoid being seen by any prospectors.

"We have no choice, this is really bad. Pretty sure that's hail," Coyote said as he stuck his hand out of the cave and pulled it back in. "See? Marble-sized hail. We're not going anywhere," he continued.

"We've got plenty of fish left smoking by the fire and that rabbit we've been slow cooking, but we'll get hungry if it's more than a couple of days. Especially, since we need to fatten you up, Skinny."

Coyote didn't care for the nickname, it always made him feel feeble. Before the hunting accident, he was strong, skilled, and a noble leader. After, he'd fallen to ground level.

"What do you want to do to pass the time? We've been on the move so much, I don't know how to sit still," Coyote said as he paced by the entrance of the cave. Sounds of hail hitting the mountains echoed with the reverberation of the thunder against the back wall of the cavern.

"We can sing, tell stories. You can tell me one of your dreams, those are always entertaining. Got a good recent one?"

"Fuck off. If we get bored enough, maybe," he answered back shortly.

"No, tell me one, things have been weird between us lately. It would be nice to hear one."

"None of them are nice, they are all dark," Coyote replied.

"Tell me the darkest one, then."

"Ok. I keep having a recurring dream where I'm trapped between two realities, but neither is of this world. I'm being cut up into pieces and then eaten by the creatures in the forest; hawks, eagles, vultures, owls..."

"Crows."

"Haha, but yes. It hurts and I can feel the pain, the tearing off my flesh being separated from bone. Then wolves, coyotes, bears, mountain lions, and foxes come by and consume me. I can't scream or cry for help. I'm all alone, you don't exist. Life here as I know it doesn't exist."

"That's wild. How often do you have it?" she asked, listening to the thunder as it grew in volume.

"Every night. Every fucking night since the accident."

35

"Damn," she uttered softly.

"Yeah. The worst part is, it doesn't end there. I still have to die. I watch my bones begin to get covered by earth and weather, then I watch as they turn to dust. I'm just trapped in time and space, wandering an endless maze until I wake up. I used to talk to our father about it and he said it was common after a near-death experience."

"Why didn't you ever tell me?"

"I don't know, it's heavy and I didn't want to burden you with my troubles. You know what's the weirdest part, though?" Coyote asked.

"What's that?" Crow answered as she glanced at her brother, the flickering of the fire dancing off the walls of the cave, creating a shimmer effect. She could sense he was pensive.

"I think I wake up from the dream, but instead I'm on a train."

"A train?"

"Yeah, it's cold and I'm alone."

"You've never even been on a train."

"I know," Coyote replied, looking down at the campfire.

"Then you have to wake up again, that sucks," Crow responded.

"I do, and every time I'm glad I'm not on that train. However, every night I go back to sleep, I wake up back on the same train."

"What's it like on the train? Outside of being cold?"

"It's empty and dark. I'm alone in this freezing boxcar, awaiting the end. I feel like I'm at death's door. All my other dreams have this extreme level of surrealism or ethereal connections to higher levels of consciousness, but this is pure void. I swear it's prophetic."

"You always say that," Crow suggested.

"This one seems like a real omen, Crow, as if it's inevitable."

"You've been through a lot, it's just a result of stress, you know? Like the way your brain reacted to the changes in your life since the accident."

"I hate calling it an accident, it was fate."

"Maybe, but was it fate or prophecy that our entire village was slaughtered?"

"No," Coyote muttered to himself.

He knew Crow was right, he'd been so wrapped up in his own demise, he hadn't allowed himself to become free of the mental confinements that came as a result of a shift in his physical state.

"We have to stay strong, awake, alert, and ready to fight at any time. I need you at your best and you still got it, Coyote. Your hatchet skills are next level and you know how to stalk and be silent like no other. Give yourself some damn credit once in a while you skinny, little fucker. I love you brother, we're in this together."

"Thanks, sis."

"This storm's got to let up by tomorrow and we can head out of here. We've been here for a bit, now it's only a matter of time before someone comes around. However, we've got to be even more careful because we're getting close to unfamiliar territory."

They were certainly not the first folks to have a campfire at that cave. After all, it was particularly high up and hard to access. It was in a very remote area and it was only a matter of time before some fool discovered it, proclaiming it as a great place to camp and start exploring. Ever since giant caves and caverns of gold were found nestled in the mountains, every mouth and entrance was doomed to become overridden with dirty scoundrels.

"You know what's funny?" Coyote continued with a bizarre smirk on his face.

"What's that?"

"I find comfort in the sounds of trains off in the distance at night when I'm sleeping."

"You're weird."

"You're one to talk. With your weird habits. You'll gut a deer, decapitate a rabbit... but when you fish you always feel sorry for the fish and their sad little eyes, as you like to call them."

"They are sad, they are so small and their little mouths make that fish mouth. It's weird, whatever. I'll *gut* you."

"Psychopath," he replied as he smiled at his sister.

"Hey, you need this lunatic around."

"I'd get by."

"Like fucking hell you would, you'd be dead in days, you skinny bastard!" she shouted with a chuckle.

Coyote laughed, watching his sister imitate what she thought life would be like for him without her. They joked around for the remainder of the night and reminisced about their mother and father.

Life had become so real so fast over the years, they seldom had time to reflect on a time of innocence and nostalgia.

"What do you think Mother would say if she were here right now?" Coyote asked.

"She'd say 'Take fucking bath in the river, Coyote, you smell like shit.'"

"Ha ha ha. You smell like shit, too, just so we're clear. No, really. What do you think she'd tell us if she were here right now, to better our situation?"

"She'd say, 'Coyote stop worrying and start living and Crow don't be so protective all the time, learn to let go.'"

"I suppose you're right, she was always optimistic."

"She was, we're nothing like her," Crow replied, snickering at the harsh reality.

She knew they were right, there was no sense in being caught up in fear and negativity, regardless of the situation. They'd found solace in the cave that evening; a feeling neither Crow nor Coyote felt in ages. As the night grew on and morning came, the storm let up and the siblings gathered the little bit of gold they had and their belongings. They headed out and over the mountain to get their buried treasure.

CHAPTER FIVE

Darkness seemed to lay like a veil for years over their village before the miners arrived. There'd been battles with settlers and fights with nearby villages over land. Crow and Coyote's people were known for being quiet, hidden, and respectful, but could turn to warriors at any given moment. Unfortunately, they were few and far between, falling victim to being solely outnumbered. They'd won battles against settlers and other villages they matched in size, however, when the miners and their families came with guns and ammunition, there wasn't much they could do.

It was in previous battles, Crow learned to kill for protection. She found she possessed a skill in turning off her rational brain and shifting straight into full-force instinct. She'd be able to go in and execute. Crow only killed in self-defense, never for pleasure or greed. She was raised to always find a resolution first and only in a state of survival would it be ok to succumb to the reigns of murder.

Her mother was a pacifist but a realist, as well. She'd named both the children and said their names had a deep meaning. Their mother was clairvoyant and came from a line of women with magic abilities.

Crow's great-grandmother was known as the Seer. She could see into the future as well as the past. She just knew things others didn't. She embodied a higher frequency, which she'd passed down to Crow. Their names, Crow and Coyote, were symbolic of that connection and were even put into the family crest.

When their mother was pregnant with the children, she had intense visions and nightmares. Some are overwhelmingly beautiful, others terrifying and morbid. She knew her children would one day have to fight on their own; she only hoped it wouldn't be true. The inevitable destiny she saw forged before her kin was dark and twisted, however, the one part she never saw clearly was the ending. She knew how things might unfold but in the end, their path was still theirs to traverse.

"With this break in the storm, we need to move fast. The weather could change again and we don't want to get trapped without a place to take shelter. Especially with it getting much colder at night," Crow stated as they trudged through the mud on the lightly worn trail.

"I move fast, you're the one that slows me down."

"Bullshit."

"Bullshit? I'm in front of you right now!"

"Only because I'm carrying more weight," Crow pointed out.

"Yeah, well, you wanted the gold."

"You'll want it, too, when we're trading for goods, food, and supplies," Crow replied.

"I just want to get to the trading post safely."

"We will, don't you worry," she insisted.

"That's kinda what I do, Crow, you know that," Coyote teased.

"Truth," she said, laughing at her brother.

The day went on and they both hiked as fast as they could to maintain a steady rate. Dusk came and they hadn't reached the site but they knew they were within a few miles, so they decided to rest up for the evening. They ate foraged food and collected water but went to sleep early as they planned to be up before sunrise.

The moon hung low in the sky as dawn came and they packed up, then headed out. The sun began to peek out from above the canopies as they descended further down the mountain. The further they went down, the further in the sky the sun rose. When they reached the site, panic began to set in. Everything looked different.

"Oh no," Crow muttered under her breath.

"A lot of trees went down during the storm," Coyote answered.

"You think? Fuck, I don't see the tree that looks like the hand but this is definitely the spot."

"Yeah, we came down the mountain and stayed relatively straight, however, with no leaves on the trees, and half of the trees on the ground, it's so hard to make sense of anything. We're going to need to climb over and under trees to move around, but I think we need to head toward the left here and search for it."

"If it went down, there's no way we'd be able to tell it apart from the others, and it could have fallen right where we buried the gold," Coyote said as wave after wave of anxiety rushed over him.

"I can't believe it, this is just our luck!" Crow yelled as she slammed her hatchet into a deceased tree in anger.

Just then, they heard the rustling of fallen leaves and limbs slowly breaking behind them.

"Hey, you two!" they heard a man yell.

Before they could process anything further, they both started running full speed ahead, weaving under and over fallen trees. Coyote's adrenaline had taken the reign and he was now charging full steam ahead of his sister. They ran for what seemed like ages through an endless array of trees until they hit the river.

"I think we lost him," Coyote said, out of breath.

"Damn, you ran fast, I simply followed your lead."

"Yeah, I don't know. I heard a voice and just took off."

"Did you get a look at him at all?" Crow asked.

"Nope. You?"

"No. Settlers or miners, most likely."

"Probably, regardless we need to be on edge tonight."

"Absolutely. We're sleeping in shifts tonight, we can't take any chances."

"Definitely," Coyote agreed.

"I should have just axed him." Crow laughed.

"He probably wasn't alone."

"I know, I was kidding. Lighten up."

"I should have bit him," Coyote said as he howled toward the sky.

"Gross, and shut the fuck up. We gotta be quiet," she insisted.

"We ran so far, we lost him way back."

"Well, let's cross the river to be safe and camp out on the other side tonight," Crow suggested.

That night, they camped out on the other edge of the river and planned their next move. They argued on whether to go back for the gold or not, then decided whoever buried it initially might be guarding a general radius of the area in hopes of catching the thief who stole their treasure. It wasn't uncommon for families to come to the area in hopes of striking it rich, so Crow and Coyote could have a slew of folks after them.

They hoped that wasn't the case.

They were fast asleep that night when they were awoken by a man in the woods with a badly bruised face, wielding a lantern in one hand and a handmade spear in the other.

"Crow, wake up someone is close by," Coyote whispered.

"What? Are you sure you aren't dreaming?" she asked quietly.

"I'm certain I saw a shadow of a man in the trees."

Crow shot up from the ground, but before she could reach for her ax, the man came stumbling out of the forest.

He dropped his wooden spear, his lantern plummeting to the forest floor beneath him as he collapsed on the ground. His face had been beaten and was swollen.

He looked as if he'd been left for dead.

"Who are you?" Crow asked the man.

He muttered a response but they couldn't make out the words. He was not a person of the nearby village like them; he was either a settler or prospector.

"He's been beaten to shit," Coyote said.

"Yeah, someone left him for dead. Hey, you got a name? What's your name?" Crow asked the man. This time growing impatient, despite the man's situation.

"Crow, he's harmless right now, he can barely walk."

"Yeah, but for all we know, this man killed our family," she responded.

"We don't know that, let's clean him up."

"Clean him up? Are you insane?" she snapped.

"No, let's get his face cleaned up and the blood off him," Coyote insisted.

"We don't need more dead weight. I'm going to put him out of his misery," Crow replied as she went for her ax.

"No, Crow, relax. He's not completely worthless."

"My name is Henry," the man uttered weakly.

"He speaks!" Crow exclaimed.

"What happened to you?" Coyote asked as he examined the man's badly bruised face.

"I was attacked by drunk miners. They beat me up, took what little money and shine I had, then took the few nuggets of gold I'd found."

"Just like everyone else around here, you're out here trying to get rich and destroying beautiful land in the process," Crow spat.

"No, ma'am, not me. I keep to myself. My mother recently died, so I've been living alone and roughing it."

"Ours too," Coyote said.

"I'm sorry to hear that. I'm sure she was a great woman like my mother. I hoped to come here and get a little bit of gold I could trade for land up north. Settle down for a while, build a home, and hunker down. I'm not trying to get rich and build an empire like the rest of these folks. They're savages," Henry said as he tried to get up from the ground.

"You just stay there for a bit," Coyote instructed.

"You're probably right. I saw you both over by the storm damage yesterday, but you ran immediately."

"That was you?" Crow inquired, keeping a steady eye on Henry.

"Yeah."

"You followed us here?" she asked again with pensive energy.

"Yes, but only because I need your help and I can make it worth your while."

Coyote glanced at his sister and interjected. "How so?"

"I have a lot of gold hidden in an abandoned cabin about twenty miles upriver. My brother-in-law and I hid gold around the home in the yard and in the walls of the cabin. There's also gold under the floorboards in the living room. If you help me get there, I'll split it with you fifty-fifty. You can take half of it, it's got to be worth over two hundred thousand dollars, easily."

"That's over four hundred pounds of gold. How do we know we can trust you? How do we know you're telling the truth?" Crow questioned.

"What am I going to do? I have nothing, no weapons, no money. My entire body hurts from being beaten and dragged."

"How do we know you're not bluffing?" Coyote asked.

"Trust me, I'm not. You gotta see it to believe it," Henry said as his eyes lit up and he cracked what little smile he could through his swollen face.

Even though they felt they shouldn't, there was something about Henry that both Coyote and Crow liked and trusted. He seemed genuine and honest, something they were not accustomed to recognizing in others.

"Where's your brother-in-law? What about him?' Crow asked.

Henry paused and was quiet for a moment, then replied, "He's dead."

"How did he die?" Coyote responded reluctantly.

"We were chopping wood at the cabin late in the summer. He went over to the wood pile to grab a big log to split. As he reached his hand down to pick up the log, a Timber Rattlesnake bit him on the hand three times very quickly."

Coyote chimed in with a grimacing look. "Wow, they are very deadly."

"Yeah, I sat with him for a couple of days while he slowly died in agony. It was horrible, there was absolutely nothing I could do for him. This place is ruthless and wild. I just want to get home with some gold. I'm willing to cut you both in fairly. Please help me."

"I think he's telling the truth, Crow."

"You might be right. So, what's in it for you then Henry?" she asked.

"Protection and the ability to access it. Otherwise, I don't think I could get there by myself. Look at me."

"Let's help him, Crow."

"Fine, we'll help you. However, you're splitting that shit fifty-fifty or I'll kill you and it won't be pretty. I'll cut your head clean off. You won't even see it coming," Crow commanded.

"I believe you. I don't want any trouble," Henry replied.

"I hope not. Well, with an extra person now, we've got to get a hunt in. We need to take a decent-sized deer down. We can get plenty of meat and hide. Henry, can you skin a deer?" Crow questioned.

"Oh, yes I can, and I'm plenty good at it."

"Good, that's what you're doing tomorrow. Coyote and I will do the stalking and hunting while you rest here, then when we're done, you can get to skinning."

"I'm happy to help out. Thank you. I mean that, those men left me for dead and these nights were getting cold. I was certain I'd become forest food."

"You're not home free, yet," Crow pointed out as she threw another log on the fire.

"Yeah, and when I get home, I'll have to break the news to my wife and family that her brother is gone."

"I hope they knew the risk," Coyote replied.

"They did, but I guess it's always easier to fantasize than to think about the harsh realities, right? I'm guilty of it myself," Henry said as he held his hand on his forehead. It was obvious he was in pain and still very much bleeding from his wounds.

CHAPTER SIX

T he sun rose yet again and a new day began to unfold as birds sang along the early morning breeze. The sky was clear, not a cloud in sight. It was warmer than it had been and the sun reflecting off the lush fern forest created a brilliant radiance that was intoxicating. The forests in the morning always had a shimmer that was gentle and unassuming, yet warm and inviting, regardless of the season. Winter was growing closer as the last little bit of autumn fluttered by.

Henry stayed at the site and rested while Crow and Coyote set out on their hunt. They knew they needed to take down a medium-sized deer. They also used every bit of the deer up, so a big deer would be more meat to keep fresh. With the warmer weather that day, there wasn't much of a chance of storing the meat unless they smoked it. They had to hope to find a family of deer, so they could find the right size. They also vowed never to kill babies or mothers with babies. They had a code and they followed it, despite the situation. They always made due.

Hours went by and they didn't see any deer. They were beginning to grow tired and called the hunt off until the next day when they spotted a family of about nine. They scoped it out and found a young buck they could take down. He'd be just the right size for meat for a few days. Plus, they could sun dry plenty for jerky without adding too much weight to their load and have enough deer skin and bones to make much-needed clothing and tools.

Coyote crept down and kept an eye on the surroundings as Crow pulled the arrow back, aiming the bow. She held her hand steady as she waited patiently. Then, in a moment's glance, she released the arrow, sending it spiraling through the cool mountain air. It hit the buck as it let out a scream. Crow loaded another arrow and fired again, repeating the process until three arrows sat buried in the young buck. Blood let out as the magnificent buck fell onto the cold earth below.

"Thank you, Spirit, for your offering," Crow expressed as she walked over to the dead deer, placing her hand over its third eye.

They brought the buck back to Henry, who now had his work cut out for him. Skinning and processing a deer was already hard enough, but adding bruised and sore hands and fingers to the mix meant Henry had it even harder.

It took him longer than usual, about four hours to complete, but both Crow and Coyote were pleased with his work. They started gathering the meat they wanted to cook right away, then the meat they were going to smoke. They began laying out the meat to smoke, then sun dry. They'd use the deerskin for shoes, however, the process took about four days of tanning the skin until it became more reminiscent of leather. It took teamwork but before long, they were all well-fed and clothed. They were ready to begin their twenty-mile hike after a week of rest.

Over that time, Henry healed up and regained strength as did Coyote, who was now fattening up some. They got to know each other well, swapping stories and playing games together. Henry was growing on them both and he was enjoying their company, as well. They set off on their hike toward the cabin.

"It should take us two days," Henry said.

"That's fair. If we keep this pace, we'll be right on schedule, I think," Crow replied.

"I just hope no one found the cabin, I mean we hid the gold well, and all, but you never know around here. Everyone has a second sense for these things. It seems they can sniff the gold out from a hundred miles away."

"No kidding," Coyote agreed.

"Ever since gold was discovered, our people and villages have suffered at extreme measures. I hate to succumb to the beast but we have nothing left at this point, we've been stripped of everything," Crow expressed.

"I'm sorry to hear that, Crow. I mean it, truly. I know you've heard my sob story already, but I do feel for you. I come from a very poor family and I understand what it's like to struggle."

"Thank you for recognizing it, at least," Crow said as she looked up at the clouds rolling in.

"You think it's going to storm?' Coyote asked Crow.

"No, maybe just light rain, we should be ok," she answered.

"I'm tired of rain, it has rained so much since I've been here," Henry muttered as he dragged his feet over the rocky terrain.

They made their way through the dense forest. The trees were bare and the sky was muted, however, everything had a deep, vibrant saturation that bled through the scenery. The last remaining leaves of fall fluttered their way to the ground as the group shuffled through the forest debris. Off in the distance, they noticed a large, black figure ahead of them. They all became anxious as they slowly approached it. Once they got closer, they were saddened by what they saw. A decapitated black bear was slumped over on the ground.

"Fucking poachers!" Crow exclaimed.

"They took just the head?" Henry asked, confused.

"Yeah, the head's the trophy for their wall at home. They leave the rest behind. This was a full-grown adult, looks like a female, too. Probably had small cubs out there."

"What a waste," Henry said as he felt deep sadness fill up inside him. Coyote remained quiet, he was always hurt by incidents like this.

"It sickens me. We honor and hold the bear very sacred in our village. We never kill bears under any circumstance," Crow said as she placed her hand over the headless bear's heart.

"They are such beautiful creatures, such a shame," Henry whispered as he wiped the tears from his eyes.

"Well, the rest of her is still in good shape. We can utilize the fur and make clothes for us. Looks like this happened yesterday, most likely. What do you think? Should we use the remnants?" Crow asked as she examined the bear.

"Works for me, I'd hate to see so much beauty go to waste," Henry said in agreement.

"I'm with Henry," Coyote concurred.

"Ok, well, it's settled. We'll take today and process the bear and we each will have a fur coat," Crow said.

"That's probably smart, the temperature is certainly dropping," Henry replied as he rubbed his hands together and blew on them to warm them up.

They took the remainder of the day to recycle the bear. They thanked the bear for providing warmth and shelter from the weather that was beginning to shift.

"You both really care for the land," Henry stated as he watched them use up every bit of the bear like a vulture cleaning the earth of decay.

"Of course, it's our home," Crow responded, slightly annoyed by Henry's statement. "See, that's the problem with you outsiders, you don't understand how to be grateful for what Earth provides for us. You only focus on the darkness around you and in turn, you bury yourself in it like shackles."

"That's true," Henry agreed.

"I mean, you came here knowing it may cost you your life right?" Crow asked.

"You're absolutely right. We knew the risks and looked where that got us. My brother-in-law is dead, I'm barely hanging on. I can't thank you both enough. I'd be dead by now if it wasn't for you."

"You're not out of the woods yet," Coyote said as he rested in the sunlight.

"Not yet, but we're close," Henry answered.

"Close isn't good enough out here, you're never home free," Crow told Henry as she finished processing the bear.

They rested that night and headed out early the next morning before the sun came up. They maneuvered their way through the hills, laughing and poking fun at Henry, how he looked in the bear fur. He continued to grow on them the more time they spent with him; they could tell he was genuine and sincere. Not like the other outsiders who destroyed their home. Regardless, they both knew deep down they couldn't totally trust him.

At any moment, he might turn on them, especially once they were close to the cabin and he felt he didn't need their protection anymore. Crow knew she needed to be alert around him, even if she let her guard down at times. Henry was so aloof and sheltered. He knew how to hunt and skin a deer but he wasn't a leader, and he certainly wasn't a killer.

He was desperate and full of hope.

Chapter Seven

Coyote awoke from the frigid nightmare, shaking. "This is getting old," he said to himself as he got up from his bed and made his way outside his home in the village.

The air was warm, it was summer and the sound of bullfrogs and cicadas filled his ears. He looked up at the moon as it hung in the night sky. Stars and meteors were abundant as the celestial doorway to the heavens undulated above him.

The Milky Way was as clear as ever, gold dust sprinkled through the sky and mixed with swirls of indigo to create a mesmerizing visual display better than any masterpiece ever created.

The land he stood on as he examined the constellations above him was sacred. His village held it in high regard and honored it with every breath. He meandered around the village thinking to himself. He enjoyed roaming the community at night and keeping watch. It was quiet and peaceful with everyone asleep.

A vibration in the ground caught his attention. He focused on it for a bit and watched as an anxious version of himself appeared before him. It was a clear copy of Coyote, right down to the eyes; they were the dead giveaway. He ran quickly toward himself but passed through the ethereal cloud copy of his being. He tried yet again and failed. It was clear he was seeing a reflection of himself in another realm.

Coyote watched himself pace in circles with extreme tension. It was unclear what was going on, but he could tell by the look on his face it was bad, very bad. The image of himself began to dissipate until it vanished altogether. This process would occur endless times throughout Coyote's life, increasing in volume as he aged. It started when he was just a baby from what he could remember, well before the accident. As far back as he could take his memory, there was always a mirror image of himself shifting around him.

No matter what he did or what he tried to think, Coyote could never understand why he was experiencing such utter disconnection from the physical realm. He seemed to be slipping through the cracks and slowly surfacing on another plane of existence.

Regardless of the place and time, he always felt as if this other part of him he was seeing was trying to get to him in the physical realm. They just could never make the complete connection. All Coyote knew was that this was a version of himself living at the same rate, he was simply in a different world. He kept this to himself, even as a child. He never told anyone, including Crow. It was his secret, something he didn't want anyone to know because of how it made him feel. He'd think it would've made him feel more connected to a distant part of himself, but it made him feel even more disconnected and lost.

"Hey Coyote, you there? Hey... hey!" Crow yelled as she snapped her fingers at him.

"What? Sorry. I was in my own world," he replied.

"Surprise, surprise. Pull out of it. Henry and I were asking your opinion. Do we push through tonight and reach the cabin before sunrise or rest this evening once the sun sets, then head out in the morning and get to the cabin by sunrise? What do you think?" Crow asked as they hiked up the incline.

"It doesn't matter to me, what do you think?" Coyote responded.

"I say we rest tonight and head out in the morning. This old logging road becomes much more strenuous and harder to navigate until we reach the top. The way down is easy. We can camp at the top and hike down in the morning. It's only about another five miles, or so, to the cabin once you come down the mountain," Henry said, obviously feeling fatigued.

"It's also getting much colder and smells like it's going to snow," Coyote added.

"I agree with Coyote, it's going to snow. Let's hike to the top and camp out tonight, then get to the cabin in the morning."

"Works for me," Henry concurred.

They would come to deeply regret the decision to camp out. The night came quickly and the crew found themselves tired and off to bed at an earlier time than usual. They were all fast asleep when all of a sudden, Coyote was awoken by sounds close to camp.

"Crow, wake up," he said but Crow didn't respond.

"Henry, wake up, someone's nearby," he whispered, however, Henry was a heavy sleeper and was off in dreamland.

Again he continued, yet neither of them woke up. He went over to Crow and shook her. "Get up now, someone is very close. I think it's a few folks."

Crow got up quickly and came to her senses.

"Henry, wake up!" Coyote said, raising his voice from a whisper but still no response from Henry.

As Coyote went over to wake him up, they heard a gunshot. Someone fired a pistol into the air to wake them up. Before Coyote and Crow could process the sounds, they took off into the dark wilderness as Henry scrambled to come to. When he did, it was too late and he'd been captured by the four men who'd been stalking their campsite. The men grabbed Henry and bound him at his hands and feet, forcing him back to their campground.

Crow and Coyote ran a good mile away but turned around to go back for Henry after they hid out for a while. Once they got close, they knew Henry's chances of survival were rapidly diminishing to nothing.

They watched from the shadows, perched on an outcropping from above as the men interrogated him. They were too far away to make out every question but they could tell they were asking about gold.

"I recognize two of the men," Coyote said, watching with great intensity.

"The short fat man and the tall, skinny, bearded fellow are the two we saw burying the gold. They found us," he continued.

"Maybe they don't know us and they are ransacking any campsite they can find asking questions?" Crow suggested as they observed the men shove Henry on the ground and kick his face toward the earth.

"They're going to kill him!" Coyote exclaimed.

Suddenly, the man with the long beard yanked Henry up and pointed a shotgun into the back of his head. Henry was shaking and silent, however, his fear was palpable filtering through the early morning forest. The sun was slowly rising from the horizon and the birds were beginning their morning serenade.

"No," Coyote howled as the man pulled the trigger. Henry hit the forest floor. The bullet went right into his head, as blood pooled out from under him. Henry was dead. The men had shown no mercy.

"You hear that?" one of the men asked as they shined their lanterns toward the edge of the shadows.

"Shut up, you'll get us killed," Crow whispered to Coyote. Tears filled her eyes.

"We need to get out of here now and quietly," she continued, kneeling closer to the earth.

"I'll lead," Coyote said quietly, noticing snowflakes gently fluttering from the sky.

"Move very slowly," Crow instructed.

The men shuffled their feet toward the rockline and looked up at the outcropping, but it was still too dark to see the siblings. The sky grew in light as the dark of night settled and a new day began. Crow and Coyote found themselves yet again met with tragedy and grief.

There seemed to be no escaping it.

CHAPTER EIGHT

"We can't keep going at this rate!" Coyote yelled at Crow as they made their way into the night.

"We don't have a choice. This is our life. It's harsh, but we need to make the best of it. We always do," Crow replied, feeling stubborn and jaded.

"We're going to die, either both of us or one of us. Our time is running out and we're reaching the end. Something's got to give."

"We have a good amount of the gold. If we can just get to Signal Mountain, then we can trade gold for goods, maybe even purchase our own land and figure out a fresh life for ourselves."

"That's wishful thinking."

"Call it what you want, but I'd rather keep living than give up like you have," Crow snapped.

"I haven't given up, I'm just a realist," Coyote shot back at his sister.

"You *have* given up, Coyote. Ever since the accident, you've felt sorry for yourself."

"Fuck you, Crow. You don't know what it's like for me. I feel like I'm deadweight. That you'd be better off without me."

"Is that what you think? I don't want to do this without you, you're all I have. I know I'm rigid and hard on you at times, but I love you so much, Coyote. I can't do this without you, we're a team."

"I love you, too."

They hugged one another and took a moment to hold each other close. Although they were quick to squabble and disagree at times, they were always just as quick to be there for one another when one of them needed support. The sense of resolution brought a calming feeling between the two siblings and they continued foraging for food further down the ridge line.

"We still have a few hours until the sun rises. It looks like we can make it down toward the valley soon if we press on. What do you want to do, Skinny?" Crow asked as she peered down the pathway and examined the trail ahead of them, using the moonlight as her guide.

"Let's keep rolling and get to some grass and flatter ground," Coyote responded.

"Sounds good to me. We can find a safe place to catch some rest once we reach the bottom," Crow mentioned, straightening her back to stretch.

"I don't know if I'll sleep tonight. I feel like shit about what happened to Henry. He was one of the good ones and that's rare around here."

"I feel bad, too, but there is nothing we could've done. We were ambushed in our sleep. It's unfortunate. Once we get to the valley, we can do a ceremony for him. It's only right."

"Ok, that would be nice," Coyote agreed.

"It's just a couple more miles if that, we'll be at the bottom soon."

They continued their march down the mountainside. Constellations, meteors, and planets twinkled in the night sky.

"We're getting close to Black Nightcaps; I can smell them," Coyote whispered.

He had a second sense for the hallucinogenic mushroom. Black Nightcaps were a highly potent and irresistible psychedelic fungus that grew in very late and early winter in the Appalachian mountainsides. They liked to grow at the base of Hemlock trees and would create abundant fairy rings throughout the forest during that time of year. They were incredibly enticing and every man, woman, and animal had a hard time resisting them.

The Nightcaps reached about nine inches in height. They had long skinny stems and big pointy caps, resembling a witch's hat, and could create elaborate and intricate visuals that produced magnificent waves, which rippled through the body. The high would last about eight hours, depending on how much a person ate.

Some folks got caught up in consuming them and would devour an entire ring, in which case the effects could last a day or two. There were stories of men getting lost in the woods for a week because they were high on Nightcaps. Most found their way out and eventually sobered up from the experience, but there'd been reported deaths.

It wasn't necessarily the mushrooms people had to watch out for, rather the guardians that protected them and acted as gatekeepers for the fungi. They might not always be seen, but they could be heard. Wherever there were Nightcaps, the guardians were found. The guardians were known as the Mechanized Elves. They were little, pale men with weathered skin and black, pointed hats that looked identical to the fungi. They had long, gray beards with giant wide eyes and wore red shirts with red pants and black boots. They were nocturnal beings who could be benevolent, but they also were tricksters and they'd take full advantage of people when they were in their fragile and vulnerable state, high on Nightcaps. People often got misguided by them and were led to areas of the wilderness, which they might not return from.

"Are you sure you smell them?" Crow asked.

"You know I do, it's like a sixth sense. Besides, they don't affect me like most."

"Yeah, I know you love them."

"I enjoy the state they put me in and the visuals they create, but like everyone else, I have to look out for the elves," he replied as they paused on the trail for a moment. "They like to fuck with me just as they do with other people."

"They mess with me more," Crow interjected.

"Oh, they do. I don't know what it is about you, however, they seemed to really love screwing with you."

"They just like to play endless games, fucking tricksters. Let's move quickly and both try to resist them," Crow said as she felt a sense of uncertainty come over her. She knew it was extremely rare to make it through the forests without eating them if they were within eyesight.

"The scent is getting stronger, can you smell them?"

"Not yet, I hope you're wrong, Coyote."

They turned the bend and the landscape began to level out, the trees now mostly evergreen Hemlock trees. Ferns and lichen decorated the forest floor as they etched their way through the woods.

"Look at that ring!" Coyote exclaimed.

"Keep moving, Skinny!" Crow shouted at her brother.

Crow continued on further and after a moment or two, realized Coyote wasn't with her. She spun around and started backtracking. When she found him, he was on his hands and knees consuming Nightcaps.

"Damn it, Coyote, let's go before you get sucked in by the elves."

Coyote got up and made his way toward his sister, but before he could even take a few more steps, he succumbed to the desire to devour the rest of the mushrooms in the ring. Crow ran to grab her brother when a voice in the distance caught her attention. It was quiet and high-pitched. She tried her best to ignore it, but the voice was now getting louder and more harmonious. Before she could reach Coyote, the singular sound now was joined by a choir that was increasing in volume. It was too late, it was the Mechanized Elves.

They began to sing and chant, "Enter the ring, hear us sing, enter the ring, hear us sing," over and over. They started to stack and layer voices on top of each other, their machine-like bodies advancing like robotic drones.

Black Nightcaps began to spread out along the ground. In unison, the elves all looked up at Crow and exposed their beards and wide eyes. They moved like gadgetry as if something was controlling them with a remote. The elves sang and danced, moving methodically and mechanically. She was transfixed.

They continued to belt out, "Enter the ring, hear us sing."

Crow dropped to the earth and started eating all the mushrooms she could. Before they knew it, the siblings had eaten three full rings. They were in for it. The elves continued to perform and chant while Crow and Coyote fell into a deep psychedelic state.

They both lay on their backs as extreme colors and hues vibrated off the trees and forest floor. Intricate geometrical patterns filled their eyes as they began to see energy fields extend from them and outward into the surrounding wilderness.

The details of the images in their minds were vivid and complex. They both began to drift to sleep and enter a soma-like state. The little, bearded elves gathered simultaneously into a cluster and at once carried Crow and Coyote off into the shadows of the thicket. Behind closed eyelids, they both were in a multiverse of cosmic entities and multi-dimensional beings.

Nightcap mushrooms had an uncanny ability to transport the mind to other realms and realities. Most entered the lower realm where they were met by a myriad of primordial gods and goddesses who each possessed a particular dimension they occupied as well as a vibration they resonated at. In the lower realms, it was a lower frequency, in a higher realm a higher frequency. Although the elves had high-pitched voices, they were part of the lower realm.

No one knew for sure if the Mechanized Elves were real or if they were a product of the fungi. They were said to live in evergreen trees and act as mycological protectors of the Nightcaps and their mycelium. Their role was to guide and tend the mycelium as it stretched its way through the Appalachian floor. They worked hard every night to carve pathways in the soil for the mycelium to expand and flourish. Then, when the mushrooms fully matured, they waited for travelers to pass by and consume the fungi, so they could play tricks on them.

Crow and Coyote were deeply lost in a blanket of complex dreamwork and lucid landscapes. The high continued for hours and hours as they both moved deeper into the folds of lunacy.

Crow entered a world of darkness, while Coyote, on the other hand, shifted into a universe of interconnected beauty. It was the only time in his life, he truly felt deeply connected to the earth. With all the darkness around them, the mushrooms gave him a chance to unravel and become rooted in the sky. He felt that was the message the Nightcaps transmitted. The problem was, most folks were too consumed by the world around them to fully let go and embrace the experience.

The siblings traveled further and further down the rabbit hole. A full day went by and it wasn't until the following morning, they came out of it and found themselves safely at the bottom of the mountain.

They were asleep in a valley surrounded by a cluster of white trilliums. Coyote let Crow sleep a while longer.

"You awake, Crow?" Coyote finally asked.

"I'm coming out of it. Is it morning?" she asked as she slid her hand across her face and let her eyes adjust to the light.

"Yeah, but you slept for a full day. I've been keeping an eye on you for over twelve hours. We were carried off by the elves and carefully looked over before they dumped us in the valley. I talked to them. They were nice but they're always friendly with me."

"I must have eaten a ton to be out for a full day," Crow muttered as she rubbed her eyes.

"You ate at least a whole ring. How'd it go, are you ok?" he inquired.

"Yeah, I'm ok, but it got dark and scary. I was kidnapped by the Fleshcrawler."

The Fleshcrawler was a human who during trying times, decided to consume human flesh as a means of survival. It, in turn, was cursed to walk the mountain range, seeking an insatiable hunger for human meat. It fed off of evil and stalked the innocent, although if it got hungry enough it would feed off of anyone and anything. It was skinny to the point of starvation and crawled swiftly on its hands and feet like an animal. Its skin was pale and tight. Its blue veins were visible pumping under its translucent flesh. Its ribs protruded out sickly and gaunt; a grotesque figure with a sewn mouth and big soulless eyes. Its head was bald and ears pointy, abnormally small in comparison to its skull.

The Fleshcrawler was known to unravel its threaded mouth to expose its giant, sharp teeth. It thrived off of dark energy and could travel deep into the mind and automate the psyche of those it chose. The Fleshcrawler played games to mimic the sound of friends and loved ones. It also liked to pretend to be lost travelers or people in distress in disguise. It earned its victim's trust, then consumed them at any given time of its choosing.

"What happened?" Coyote asked nervously.

"He just ate me, plain and simple. He devoured every bit of me until there was nothing left, and there was nothing I could do about it."

"That's scary. But the Fleshcrawler can't get us, Crow, you know that. As long as we both have the amulets around our necks, then we'll always be safe from the likes of the creature. It's the other forms of unspeakable evil that threaten us, now."

"I know, he just really creeps me out. He has ever since we were kids and we saw him in the woods stalking us," she insisted.

When Crow and Coyote were younger, they were playing at home in the forest late one evening. They saw a little boy about their age, who asked if he could play with them. They welcomed him to join them and the children enjoyed each other's company for a while, playing various games. The boy lured them deeper into the woods before he transformed into the Fleshcrawler.

Their father showed up just in time as the creature had both kids pinned to the ground and had its tentacle arms over their throats as it was beginning to unravel its mouth. Their father hit it with a hatchet and the thing screamed, running off into the night.

Later that evening, their parents gave them their amulets. They were simplistic, a golden pendant for each of them. Crow's, of course, had a crow on it, and Coyote's, a coyote. They were crafted by both of their parents with immense love and care.

They were presented with their gifts and told they must be worn at all times to keep them safe from harm. From that day forward, they were never stalked or attacked by the Fleshcrawler again.

That didn't mean they couldn't see it moving swiftly through the forest or hear its faint cries for help and animalistic screams during the dark of night. They did, everyone around there did. The Fleshcrawler moved fast and covered much ground on any given night.

It was not uncommon to find remnants of its victims' entrails and body parts scattered throughout the Appalachian wilderness.

"We're safe, Crow. As long as we have these, we are okay," Coyote whispered to his sister as he held his talisman close to his heart.

Crow put her head on her brother's shoulder for a moment. It was rare he felt like his sister needed him, however, in that moment it was clear she was just as dependent on him as he was on her. They were a team and despite their issues at times, they always worked together.

"I honestly don't know what I'd do without you, Skinny," she said softly as she closed her eyes and rested longer.

Coyote sat there, continuing to watch over his sister. The sun slowly began to rise as the dawn chorus started to sing through the early morning air. He shifted and placed his hand on her cheek.

"Crow, wake up, we gotta get moving. The sun is starting to rise."

"Thanks for letting me get some extra rest, you never really sleep on those Nightcap trips. My brain needed it. Time to keep moving north," she murmured as she gathered herself and stood up to greet the daylight.

"We're in the valley and out in the open once we step out of these woods. We need to be extra alert and aware today. What's that smell, do you smell that?" Coyote said.

"Watch out, Coyote!" Crow screamed at the top of her lungs, interrupting Coyote, who was oblivious to the fact he was about to step on a severed foot.

CHAPTER NINE

"What the hell?!" Coyote exclaimed, jumping into the air in surprise. Crow peered around and noticed more human body parts.

"Look, there's a hand and another foot."

"And another hand," Coyote replied, incredibly mortified.

They approached the edge of the forest. Where the woods line met the valley was a stack of severed limbs.

"This is horrifying," Coyote muttered as they carefully made their way past the hands and feet rotting on the cold ground.

"Holy shit, look up!" Crow shouted.

When her brother glanced above, he was met by the sight of the three skeletons hanging in a tree. They all appeared to be prospectors. Two of the men were young, late teens, and the other man was older and bearded. By the looks of it, they'd been there for a while as they were heavily decomposed. It appeared like something, maybe the Fleshcrawler, had been feasting off them.

"Let's get out of here!" Coyote yelled and the two quickly made their way past the corpses into the valley. The sky was now filled with purple and orange hues as the sun continued to rise from the horizon.

"I'm starving. We need to eat, Skinny."

"No kidding," Coyote replied, his stomach rumbling.

"We should be able to get some fishing and trapping in today. Catch some rest and recoup from the Nightcap journey, then we can really focus on heading north."

"I'm all for a day to fish, trap, and catch some rest. I spent the better part of the last day watching over you while you were knocked out."

"I appreciate it so much, brother."

Just then, they heard a scream echo through the valley. As they continued further through the pasture, they approached a small hunting cabin.

"The screams are coming from inside that cabin," Coyote told his sister as she scanned the area around them. They both listened closely as the yells continued.

"Sounds like a woman," Crow whispered.

"Should we help her?"

"I think we should keep moving on. We can't get caught up in someone else's problems. After all, we don't know who she is."

"I'm going to check it out, I'll be right back."

"Damn it, Coyote," Crow hissed.

He ran over to the side of the cabin and peeked his head into the window to see a young woman with dark brown hair and delicate freckles sprinkling her porcelain skin. She was in distress. She was tied to a bed and appeared to have been beaten. She was alone in the cabin and there was no one in sight around the area. Coyote made his way to the front of the cabin carefully and surveyed the farmland surrounding it. It was quiet and desolate. He ran into the one-room house and untied her from the bed. Her face was swollen and she was bleeding from her nose and mouth.

"Thank you so much. You are an angel from god," the woman cried out as Coyote freed her from the binding. Crow came running into the cabin.

"What the hell, Coyote? Are you trying to get us killed?" she yelled at him.

"It's ok, she's alone."

"I can't thank you enough. My name is Lorna. A man, I don't know his name, kidnapped me and brought me out here on his wagon. This is his cabin. Then he beat me up and raped me."

"Where is he now?" Crow asked.

"I don't know, he got me blacked out drunk on shine. When I woke up, he was gone."

They heard a rustle outside, then the man came barging in. He was big and burly with a thick, black mustache and handlebar sideburns. He reeked of moonshine and instantly ran at Crow. Before he got two feet into the cabin, she struck him right between the eyes with her hatchet. He hit the wood floor and it reverberated throughout the room. His body convulsed as he lay in a pool of blood. Lorna screamed, then fell silent as Crow and Coyote dragged the man's body out and hid it behind the cabin.

"How can I ever repay you?" Lorna asked the siblings.

"Is there any food here?" Crow answered.

"There is!" she exclaimed, scrambling to the cupboard.

They made eggs and bacon with grits and large chunks of crusty bread. The trio ate all the food they could and filled their bellies.

"Lorna, I see there's a horse outside. Can I borrow it?" Crow asked.

"Of course."

"I think I have a plan. Coyote, you and Lorna stay here. I'm going to horseback ride around the left side of the valley and make my way back to where the gold is buried. I can take a day to locate it, remove what we need, then bury it again. I'll draw a map this time and come back with the gold. We can head to Signal Mountain from there. What do you think, Coyote?"

"How long will it take? What if you don't find it? How do you know we're safe here or that you'll be ok on your own?" Coyote asked nervously.

"It will take me two days, tops. If I can get out there quickly and make a day to look for it, I can find it. I know I can, I just need a day or so. Lorna, we'll give you gold for your horse."

"The horse isn't mine, you can have it. I need to get back to Gold City, though."

"You can ride with us, we'll drop you off close to town. Coyote and I must stay on the outskirts."

"Alright, that works for me. I'm so grateful for you both. That man probably would've continued to have his way with me until he killed me."

"Vile scum," Coyote replied, glaring through the window at the dead man in the snow.

"The hills are unfortunately full of them now, but their time will come," Crow told them with confidence.

"Be safe, sis, I love you."

"I love you, too, Skinny, and I'll see you in a couple of days." She headed out and left Coyote and Lorna at the cabin, making her way back toward the treasure.

"What will you do once you get to town?" Coyote asked Lorna.

"I honestly don't know. I came here for a better life from overseas. I'm from the Highlands of Scotland. My family came here a few years ago and settled in the mountains of North Carolina. I traveled with my sister, her husband, and their children to Gold City in hopes of making some money and buying land.

"We'll give you some gold for the horse, you can use it to buy whatever you want."

"Coyote, you and Crow are a godsend. Bless you both. I thought I was certainly going to die alone and tied up in this cabin."

"How did you meet the man?"

"My brother owns a saloon in town, we met there briefly before he kidnapped me and brought me out here a few days ago."

"Well, you're safe, now. Crow and I'll get you back to your family."

Evening came and the temperature began to drop. They gathered wood for the fireplace and built a cozy fire. They spent the better part of the night getting to know each other and discussing the dark energy that surrounded the mountainside.

"Do you hear that, it sounds like someone outside?" Coyote asked.

"I don't hear anything."

"Ok, maybe it's just the wind howling, it's really ripping out there," he replied.

They could hear the tin rooftop shaking above them.

"I'm going to get more logs from the front porch," Lorna said as she stepped outside. She went out into the cold night air while Coyote stayed by the fire, hatching a plan.

Lorna came back into the cabin. "There's a little boy outside, he says he's looking for his family. He's lost and needs my assistance."

Coyote went outside and gazed around. "I don't see a little boy."

"He's right there, he asked me for help." She pointed over toward the oak tree about thirty feet from the porch

"I don't see a little boy, Lorna." Chills ran down Coyote's spine as he realized what was going on. "Get inside."

He grabbed Lorna and pulled her into the cabin, slamming the door behind them, then placed the dresser behind it. "Hold this amulet around my neck in your hands, we will be safe."

She wrapped both her hands around the pendant, clasping it tightly in her grasp. "What is that thing outside?" she asked, her voice tight with fear.

Coyote looked to see the Fleshcrawler peering into the window. Voices began to ping and dance around the cabin. They could hear the sounds of children laughing and the faint whispers of lost loved ones. The creature screamed and yelled when it didn't get its way. It jumped on the roof and began banging on it violently before leaping back on the ground and bolting to the window to unravel its sewn mouth and expose its sharp teeth.

Lorna cried out in horror.

"It's the Fleshcrawler. Trust me, as long as you ignore its cries for help and stay here close to me, clenching this charm, you'll be ok. We'll make it through the night."

The echoes of its shrieks continued well into the night until sunup. Crow arrived late that afternoon, much earlier than they anticipated. Coyote and Lorna were both grateful after their experience the night prior. When Crow returned, however, she didn't have good news. She'd located the chest and retrieved the gold, but on her way back to the cabin, she was ambushed by the men they stole from.

"They have the entire family and some hired guns after us. I only got away cause that is one fast horse. I did some thinking on the trip and think we should have Lorna do the trading for us in Gold City. We can get whatever we need in town. Then, we can make the trek with goods and money in hand to Signal Mountain where we can look at getting our own land and settling down for a bit. What do you think, Lorna? We can pay you in gold fairly for the risk you'd be taking, we have a lot of it."

Lorna considered the proposal, then nodded. "I accept your offer."

"That is great news. It's settled, then. We'll head out this evening and should arrive in town by dawn."

Chapter Ten

They arrived in Gold City by morning. Lorna went to the downtown square to her brother's saloon, while Crow and Coyote stayed on the outskirts of town, hiding in the pine forests.

When she walked into the bar, her brother was thrilled to see her. "Lorna, there you are! Where have you been? We've been so worried about you. Oh my god, your face! What happened to you?" he asked, putting his arms around his sister in an embrace.

"Malcolm, I'm so happy to see you! You know that piece of shit from the other night, the one with the huge mustache and suspenders that was hanging around? Who wouldn't leave me alone? He kidnapped me and took me out to his hunting cabin."

"Where is he? I'll kill the son of a bitch!" he said, as he clenched his fists, peering behind his sister to see if he saw the man nearby.

"He's thankfully dead. He'd tied me to the bed and beat me up, but two siblings traveling in the area heard my screams and rescued me. They killed him. Listen, I need to speak to you in private. Can we go into the back?" she asked her brother as she whispered in his ear.

"Of course, follow me," he answered as he led her past the bar patrons to the backroom, closing the door behind them.

"What's going on?" he asked.

"The brother and sister who saved me have some gold to trade."

"To trade? We don't have anything to trade right now, all I have is liquor."

"They're nomads and can't travel in this area without risk of being killed and robbed. They need our help to barter for goods and are willing to pay us in gold. They also gave me some for that piece of shit's horse," she explained while showing her brother a big gold chunk Crow traded her for the burly fellow's stallion.

"Lorna, that's huge!"

"I know, and they have plenty more to offer us if we help them out. Can you come with me to meet them on the outskirts of town?" she asked quietly.

"Yes, let me get James to watch the saloon while we're gone," he answered with a look of bewilderment in his eyes.

Their family had been through difficult times just like everyone else. Malcolm only had the bar due to a loan he'd received with an incredibly high-interest rate. He feared that his life may even be in danger if he didn't come up with more money fast enough to pay off his debts.

When they reached the edge of town, Crow and Coyote were waiting patiently for them and were excited to meet Malcolm to get his help.

"I can't thank you both enough for rescuing my sister. You're both angels. Thank you. I'm happy to return the favor," Malcolm told them.

They discussed a deal and what Crow and Coyote needed, giving Lorna and Malcolm gold to exchange. They decided they'd meet at Malcolm's house outside of town that evening to make the exchange of goods.

Later, they all met at the home and Crow and Coyote gathered their goods and provisions. Malcolm and Lorna had traded the gold for another horse, dried beans, rice, corn grits, oats, and a plethora of odds and ends. Crow and Coyote gave Lorna and Malcolm a substantial amount of gold for their help. Enough to pay off Malcolm's debt, as well as purchase land for both him and Lorna. They said their goodbyes as Crow and Coyote headed out of town into the dense Appalachian wilderness.

They'd managed to make it to Gold City safely and make the exchange without a hitch, much to their surprise. They'd expected the old man and his family would've caught up to them by now. They considered themselves fortunate and found a desolate spot deep in the forest where they could camp out and rest for a few days. They needed to eat, sleep, and relax. They'd been on the go for a year, dodging thieves, bootleggers, and murders.

"What do we do now, Crow? We have goods, horses, and gold left over. We can't hang around here too long. The men and their families are bound to catch up to us."

"We need to get far away from here. We can make the trek to Signal Mountain in a couple of days. We should be safe out here for the next two days. I high-tailed it out there and made major headway on them. I'm confident they're way behind and possibly even completely off our scent by now. We got to Gold City without an issue, we're doing alright," she replied while stirring the rice and beans cooking in the pot over the campfire.

"I'll take your word for it, sis. I need to rest and eat. I've been feeling weak and tired. I'm needing some good sleep tonight," Coyote responded.

"Let's eat, take it easy this evening. Go to bed early."

"Sounds good to me," he answered with a yawn.

They ate and went to sleep quickly. Both siblings finally had a moment to relax and unwind. They slept peacefully through the night and by morning they both felt well rested. They spent that day fishing, laughing, and telling stories; reminiscing about their family and village. It was the best the two felt in a very long time. The next night approached and they repeated the process. They ate rice, beans, and fish by the fire and swapped ghost stories.

Ever since they were kids, they loved to share tales of folklore and ancient mythology. Their people had an abundance of fables that depicted various beings and creatures. Most of them were real tales of creatures like the Fleshcrawler or the Mechanical Elves.

While others portrayed stories of mythical beings whose existence had never been proven. Two of those particular narratives are the tale of the Moss People and the Legend of the Nomad. The two sagas were Crow and Coyote's favorite mostly because, unlike the others, they seemed to be based on fantasy and fiction.

"The Legend says the Nomad emerged from the ripple of darkness that gave birth to the Appalachian mountains millions of years ago and was cursed to wander the rugged landscapes for eternity," Crow said as she told the tale of the Nomad. The wind rustled through the trees as the branches creaked and screeched in the cold night sky. She continued weaving the story.

"The Nomad traverses the craggy ravines and steep hillsides of the mountains, desperately seeking someone to consume, so that he can take their place in this realm and subject them to his eternal punishment. He lurks in the Appalachian wilderness, stalking travelers and mountain folk. He is extremely tall and slender. He has a head of antlers which are entangled in a pile of moss, lichen, ferns, and forest debris. The red glow of his tiny eyes can be seen passing through the forests at night. He's a shapeshifter and can present himself as a human or animal in order to gain trust before he steals your soul and condemns you to a world of pure isolation and loneliness," Crow narrated.

Coyote interrupted the story, his brow knitted with concern. "I feel bad for the Nomad. He didn't choose to be a loner, he just emerged from the darkness when the mountains formed, much like the Moss People and Sasquatch. What a sad life to live, alone and desperately seeking a friend or companion. I don't think the Nomad is as evil as everyone says, Crow."

"Me either. Ever since we were kids and mother would tell the story, I always felt an overwhelming feeling of sorrow and despair for him," she agreed as she looked up at the fully lit moon above.

"You know, I saw him once when we were kids," Coyote mentioned as the flames of the fire danced off his face.

"Sure you did, Skinny."

"I'm a serious, Crow. The night of the hunting accident when Father cut my arm off to free me from the boulder, I saw him in my mind's eye. I believe he is a benevolent creature and he saved me that night. Somehow. I'm sure of it. Maybe he was there and helped drag me out of the raging river. That night, I felt this pull that was so severe, it seemed otherworldly. I don't know, maybe it's all in my head," Coyote said as he hung his head low.

"The legend says he can be right beside you without being seen, so maybe he *was* there that night. It's a miracle you survived and I'm so grateful you did, brother."

"It was just so vivid and clear. I was being submerged underwater and gasping for air, then everything went black. I began to leave my body. I found myself floating above the river. I observed you and Father struggling in a panic to break me free before Father had to cut me loose. When my arm severed from my body, I immediately was brought back to this plane of existence. Right before I made the return, I saw the Nomad guide me out of the water."

"Why have you never told me this?" Crow exclaimed.

"I don't know, it's one of those things you keep inside, you know? Feels good to tell you now, though."

"Coyote, I can't imagine how terrifying that experience must've been for you. You've been so tough through it all. The way you adapt to the world around you and always keep fighting, despite everything, makes me proud to be your sister."

"That means a lot to me, I love you so much, Crow," he replied as he put his arms around her.

They hugged for a moment as the wind moved through the bare tree limbs. Snow began to fall. The flurries accumulated on the forest floor and created a blanket of beauty against the naked winter wilderness. It fell harder and harder that night. They were thankful they traded for a canvas tent as it covered the roof of the makeshift shelter.

Morning approached and a quilt of white snow filled the forest throughout. They ate breakfast and fed the horses while the sun slowly rose from behind the line of evergreen trees surrounding them.

"Before we head out today, I'm going to go survey the area. We've been hiding out in this dense thicket and Rhodederon around us. We need to make sure we don't have any company on the other side of the creek," Crow said as she put on her fur from the bear they recycled, then set out. She returned about fifteen minutes later in a panic.

"We gotta hurry and get out of here. I saw footprints in the snow a quarter mile that way. We need to get going and move quietly. I don't know who it was, but we can't take any chances. I didn't hear any voices, which is concerning. They may have been watching me," she explained with a sense of anxiety in her eyes as she grasped the ax handle in preparation for an attack. She listened attentively to the sounds of the surrounding wilderness; everything was still for a brief moment.

"Over there!" a man in the distance shouted.

Before they could collect their tent, Coyote and Crow took off on horseback on the run. They managed to gather everything except a few provisions and their shelter, but it was worth it to get the extra step ahead.

They couldn't take any chances, they knew their life depended on it.

CHAPTER ELEVEN

T he sounds of horses' hooves echoed down the holler as both parties made their rapid march through the valley.

Coyote and Crow had a generous lead on the group trudging behind them. There were seven of the old man's family members trailing in anger. They had horses, a carriage, and guns. They fired a few shots at Crow and Coyote; the rings permeated the hillsides while the siblings communicated to each other where to go.

The one advantage the siblings had, was they knew the land like the back of their hands. They knew the majority of the peaks, valleys, rivers, and ravines and how to best maneuver through them.

"We're close to the hidden cave!" Coyote shouted over the stampede of horse hooves.

"I'll follow you!" Crow yelled back.

Gunshots reverberated in the valley as the family fired off another few rounds at the siblings.

"Cut across the creek," Coyote ordered.

Crow followed, her horse's feet sloshing through the crystal clear creek. Bits of sunlight shimmered off the water and to the stones below. They approached a dense and craggy outcropping. Granite boulders sprung from the base of the hillside.

"We should be safe here," Coyote whispered.

They entered the well-hidden cave. It was big and dark. They moved quietly to the back of the cavern room and gave the horses a bit of food to occupy them for a bit while they guarded the entrance and waited, poised to attack.

The cave served as a sacred meeting ground for the siblings when they were young teens. They'd discovered it one afternoon while they were out wandering the wilderness. It was their secret; they never shared the location with their parents or friends.

"Look, the crow I painted is still here," Crow said.

"So is my coyote," Coyote replied, pointing at the faded drawing.

"I remember the day we painted them," Crow responded, feeling reminiscent of a time when they were not under constant threat.

"That was a fun day. I miss those days. No fear, no turmoil. I remember coming home and seeing Mother and Father, then celebrating Mother's birthday."

"That's right, it was her birthday," Crow murmured, keeping a close eye on the entrance, ready to pounce at any second.

"We were in the forest looking for blackberries for her birthday pie. That was the day we found the cave."

"I miss them so much."

"Me too," Coyote said faintly while he observed the sunlight peeking through the cavern door. A few hours rolled by and it was clear they must have lost the family, so were safe to take shelter in the cave for the night. While they were gathering food and supplies from the horses, something on the wall caught Crow's eyes.

"Hey, Coyote, check this out."

Coyote made his way through the dimly lit space to the cavern wall. "That's interesting," he replied, peering closer. "It's a drawing of the Nomad. Look, that's his crown of antlers and forest debris. His long, slender body with elongated fingers and stretched-out legs. You can see feathers and other forest matter hanging from his body."

It was clearly a painting of the Nomad. It was clean and precise. The line work was chaotic yet unified.

"Who do you think could have drawn it?" Crow asked as she ran her fingers over the stone and felt the paint that saturated the rockface. The paint was jet black and appeared to have been there for years. "How did we never see this?" She lifted her lantern to the wall, examining the painting further.

"We never came this far back for too long. We also stayed close to the entrance. I mean, we only ever came here a handful of times."

"So, who would have painted it and why?"

"Maybe someone was camping here and had an encounter with the Nomad," Coyote answered, his face fixated on the glyph.

"Possibly. Maybe this is proof he is real."

"I liked to think so," Coyote concurred.

They spent the night in the cave and reflected on their childhood, talking about the good times with their friends and family, whom they missed deeply.

"I feel like I'm harping on the same thing, but I'm worried, Crow. The future will catch up to us, it's inevitable. We still have a week of travel on horseback to get to Signal Mountain."

"We've made it this far, I'm sure they are a long way away from us, now. We turned them to dust in the valley on the horses and there's no way they'll locate the entrance. They would've come in here and shot us dead if they knew where we were. We're trapped in here with nowhere to go."

"Should we hang here for a few days?" Coyote asked reluctantly.

"We can, we are safe but we lost some provisions back at the campsite. We'd have to venture out in a few days, however, it's only buying us a small amount of time and slowing down the journey north. We need to get to safer ground, a place where we know we can meet up with our own people. Move forward with our life."

"You're right, we can't stay here forever. Let's head out tonight," Coyote replied.

"I'm going to stash the map in this little nook that's here on this part of the cave wall." Crow placed her hand at the hole and reached into the crevice. "I'll hide it here. If they catch up to us, they'll have to keep us alive and take us to the cave to get the map. They'll need us alive even with the map to find it, trust me. All they want is their treasure and we're useless to them if we're dead and they don't have it," Crow said with confidence as she tucked the map into the cavern crevice.

"Which way should we go when we get out to the clearing?" Coyote inquired as he watched Crow carefully hide the map.

"We'll head northeast. We can go out to the creek, follow it to the river and stay along the waterline. We'll be able to stay hidden but keep track of where we're going. We can come back for the map in the early spring if we don't run into the scoundrels first. We have enough gold to help us trade and get through the winter and spring, but I don't want to risk searching for the cave and the gold in the summer because of the overgrowth. Maybe all the fools will be gone by then," Crow answered while loading up provisions onto her horse's back.

They silently walked out of the cave, down the creek toward the river. Once they reached it, they followed it north in the direction of Signal Mountain. The trek through the rough wilderness was difficult on horseback and would take a couple of weeks, but if they could get there safely, they could trade and find a place to stay and work.

The river snaked and carved its way into the rolling green hills that encased it while the pair rode alongside it for a few days. On day four, they were greeted by a wood-covered bridge. It was built for train tracks. They decided to rest there for a bit early one afternoon. The sun was vibrant in the crystal clear sky. There wasn't a cloud in sight, making the sky a striking blue. As they sat there resting and feeding the horses, they had the idea to break away from the river and follow the train tracks north.

The terrain was easier to walk and they could cover more ground faster, especially on horseback. If a train came by, they could duck into the forest to hide out. They followed the tracks for another day when a huge cold front rolled in. Clouds gathered and it began to snow as the temperature plummeted. The snowflakes descended at a rapid rate, so the siblings decided to set up camp away from the tracks to wait out the storm.

They found a rocky overhang nearby where they could take cover and be out of anyone's visibility on the train or the tracks. The flurries fell and grew in size as the snow covered the woods quickly. Crow built a small fire and they ate some rice, beans, and fish in silence. Nightfall drew near and the moon hung in the clouds as stars slowly popped out and glimmered overhead. Both of them drifted off to sleep, while the snow continued to pile up around them. It was dead quiet, all that could be heard was the faint sounds of the tree limbs shifting against one another. Then all of a sudden, Coyote shot up from his sleep.

"Crow, wake up. Crow... Crow, wake up! I hear something. I have a bad feeling," he said, scanning the woods around him.

Crow was in a deep sleep and did not respond. Coyote stood up and gathered his senses. He could hear something or someone near them.

"Crow!" he screamed as he felt two men grab him and put a burlap sack over his head. He tried to cry out again for Crow, but she was fast asleep.

The men tied Coyote up and made their way to Crow, who was about a hundred feet away from them. Before they could reach her, though, she was up on her feet with her hand on her ax handle, ready to fight. The man pointed a gun at

Crow as the bearded fellow ran off into the shadows with Coyote.

"We have your brother tied up!" the man shouted as the wind howled and snow cascaded from the night sky.

"If you hurt him, you'll never find your treasure. I'll give what I have back to you and tell you where the rest of your gold is. The skull, too, but we must make a deal first," she yelled, the ax grasped tight.

"I don't trust you savages," the man spat.

"Savages? You all are the savages, you've destroyed this area and given evil something to feed off of!" she exclaimed. The moon hung over her shoulder as she stood there full of anger. "I'll put my weapon down. Here's some of the gold. I've buried the rest near where we found it. I have a map hidden that shows me exactly where it is. You'll need me to read and follow it, so me and my brother can find it. So, you need us both alive or you are shit out of luck," she bargained.

She placed her ax on the ground and removed the satchel around her waist, tossing it toward the man. He pulled out hunks of gold. He picked her weapon off the ground and demanded she get in front of him. The man shoved the rifle into Crow's back, forcing her into the inky darkness.

"I want to see my brother before we make the journey. I need to know he's alive," she said with her arms up in the air.

The man brought her brother over and yanked the sack roughly off Crow's head. "See? He's alive, now lead the way and they'll follow at a distance behind us."

The group followed the tracks back the way Crow and Coyote came until they reached a thin, worn pathway and turned down it. It led them to a small cabin with an abandoned train car next to it. The car was black and red, heavily rusted. The windows were busted out of the cabin and it looked dilapidated and shabby. The bearded man forced Crow into the cabin while the other men took Coyote to the boxcar and held him hostage.

"You and I'll make the ride to the map, then we'll come back here. Once we have the map, we'll untie your brother and cuff you to each other to go to the gold."

"I want my brother released, right now!" Crow demanded while clenching her fists in fury.

"No, you get us the map and we'll untie him. Or we can just kill you both now," the man replied with a sneer.

"It will take us a few days to get to it, you can't keep him tied up that long."

"Untrue, we can use more easily accessible roads that you animals can't use. We can do it in a day and a half, then be back here in a few," the man countered with intensity.

"Fine," Crow said as she sighed heavily, feeling an overwhelming sense of defeat.

Crow and the man headed out into the dawn together. The snow continued to fall but it had slowed down. She felt overwhelmed and anxious. She only hoped her brother would be alive when they returned.

CHAPTER TWELVE

C row and the old man made the ride faster than she anticipated. When they reached the cave, the entrance was full of snow. They tunneled their way through into the cavern. Crow fiddled around in the crevice and drew out the map. She handed it to the man.

He looked at it, then at her. "Good," he said before pointing the gun back at her, directing her out of the cave.

She thought about how she could kill the man right then and there, however, if she returned alone, Coyote was done for. She pushed the emotions down and obeyed the man's orders. When they returned to the cabin, she followed the man inside where he handed the map to his brother.

"It's a map, alright. It's hard to tell the general location, we'll need them to help guide us," the bearded fellow told his squatty sibling.

"Alright, then, I'll go get the bastard," the brother muttered while storming out of the cabin toward the train car to retrieve Coyote, who was alone, bagged, and tied in the frigid boxcar. Crow followed the man outside. He untied Coyote and he ran over to Crow. They hugged each other, thankful they were both still alive.

The bearded brother came out and yelled to the chubby sibling, "The carriages are ready, let's head out!"

"On with it!" the fat man screamed to Crow and Coyote as he shoved the rifle into Crow's back.

"Get in," he mumbled while forcing them up and into the horse-drawn carriage. The man got in after them and sat across from Crow and Coyote with his gun in hand while his brother drove the horses. The other family members followed behind in the second carriage. They traveled down the dirt roads toward the buried chest. It took a day and a half to get within a mile radius of the treasure.

"Judging by your map here, missy, we should be about a mile or so from our family's gold. Which way?" the man asked as he aimed the rifle at Crow.

"We need to go southwest toward Raven Cliff territory. There, we can follow the river to the waterfall. Once we reach the river, though, we'll have to go on foot. The paths are narrow and treacherous. It gets steep at times," Crow told them while the clouds rolled in and cold temperatures began to drop. They pulled the carriages over and the men let them out of the carriage so everyone could use the bathroom.

"What are you doing, that's not where the treasure is?" Coyote whispered to Crow, glancing at the map in her hands.

"Shut up, Coyote, you'll get us killed," she replied, her words faint.

"That's not the same map."

"I made a decoy map. I know where it is, anyway, it's in my head. They're going to kill us, regardless, when they find the gold. I have a plan to get us out of here tonight," she muttered, meeting his eyes.

"You are a crazy, Crow. It's not worth it," Coyote whispered.

"You're a fool if you don't think they plan on killing us once they get what they want. We must fight back. There's a way out."

"How? What's your grand plan? We're outnumbered," Coyote inquired as he heard the men making their way back to the carriage.

"I heard the bearded guy tell his brother he has a case of whiskey and shine for him tonight. It's the fat guy's birthday. Sounds like the whole family plans on getting drunk. I say we attack them tonight in their sleep. They'll be dead to the world. We can kill them all while they're sleeping. They may be too drunk to even wake up. It's our only chance. We have to kill them all and quickly," Crow answered.

"I don't want to live this same song and dance anymore. We have to get every one of them, once and for all," Coyote replied when the men got closer.

"Shut the fuck up, you two!" the fat man shouted in their direction.

Crow and Coyote stopped whispering and both kept their eyes on the men.

"We've decided to stay and camp here for the night. It's my brother's birthday and the whole family will be celebrating," the bearded guy told them as he guided them out of the carriage over to their tent.

"You two will sleep in here tonight. Try anything funny and we'll kill you both immediately. I won't even think twice about it," he said while he untied their hands and feet.

The sun set and the family fed Crow and Coyote, then sent them to their tent while they stayed by the fire drinking whiskey and singing songs.

"They're really drunk. Tonight is our chance, we have to move as soon as we can. We need to kill them all as fast as we can. First, I need to sneak to the carriage to find my hatchet. I saw where it is," Crow explained, her voice low.

"Are you sure about this, Crow?"

"It's our only chance, they're going to kill us, either way. Tonight, we need to attack."

"You're not wrong. Ok, I'm in," Coyote replied with uncertainty.

"Good, we'll wait until they're quiet and asleep. We'll give it an hour or so, then start with the two brothers. I'll take the fat guy, you attack the bearded brother. Then, with them both dead, we can go after the rest of the family. You kill their parents and the uncle, I'll murder the fat man's wife and daughter. After, we'll steal the horses and ride out bareback. That's the plan, you follow, Coyote?" Crow said confidently.

"It could work."

"It will, trust me," she answered.

Just then, the skinny, bearded man came staggering into the tent and grabbed Crow with his weathered hands.

"Come with me, bitch," he mumbled, slurring his words and tripping over his feet. He took Crow to the carriage and forced her into the covered area.

"Take off your clothes, now!" he demanded.

"I'm not taking off my clothes."

"Like hell, you aren't!" he yelled as he grabbed her and started trying to rip her clothes off. He held the pistol to her head.

"I'm going to either kill you or rape you. You decide," he shouted, shoving her onto the floor. He unbuckled his belt and pulled his pants down as he removed her pants. It was then in his drunken stupor, he tripped and fell over. He sat there for a moment before passing out. Crow quickly searched the covered carriage, looking for her hatchet. She fumbled around in the dark before she felt the sturdy wooden handle and lifted it off the floor.

"There you are," she murmured before she ran back to the tent. The rest of the family had retired to their tents and were fast asleep.

"You're back! What happened? I was worried sick!" Coyote exclaimed.

"Sshh, be quiet, he passed out. Now's our chance to strike. Change of plans, follow me to the carriage, so I can kill this bastard. After that, we'll kill the rest of the family, starting with the fat man and his wife. I'll get them and the daughter, you kill the uncle and grandparents."

Stepping out of the tent, they made their way to the carriage when suddenly they were attacked by the fat man and his uncle. The brother hit Coyote over the head with his rifle and the man's uncle punched Crow in the face, knocking her to the ground. She got up quickly and charged the uncle with her ax. She swung and hit him in the stomach, creating a huge gash in his side.

He began to bleed and toppled to the ground.

Crow spun around to see the fat man dragging Coyote toward the other carriage. He shoved him inside the carriage and whipped the horses as the carriage bolted down the path. Crow ran as fast as she could after them, but the carriage was too fast. She ran back to the other carriage to find the bearded fellow in a daze, falling out of it onto the snow. Without any hesitation, Crow swung the ax into his back, and he screamed in agony. She yanked the ax out and did it again, then again and again until the man was nothing but a pile of blood and guts.

"How dare you put your hands on me?" She spit on him and screamed before running back toward the other carriage, where she grabbed a horse to ride down the dirt road to find Coyote.

Crow was making great time as she could hear the carriage in the distance ahead of her as it creaked and trembled through the mountainside. The snow began to fall as she got closer to them and saw the carriage in her sight. The man led them up an abandoned logging road that traversed a mountain all the way to the top. Crow followed on horseback. The snow fell harder and the wind howled. All of a sudden, the horse she was riding collapsed to the ground. It tried to get back up but it couldn't, as it fell back on the snow.

"No, not now, please. No!" she screamed while she watched the horse take its last breath. Out of options, she pressed on up the road on foot. She noticed a shadowy figure ahead of her. It was the grandfather. She threw her ax at him, hitting him right in the heart. She turned around to see the fat man pointing a pistol at her.

"Drop the ax," he muttered while moving aggressively.

"Drop the pistol," Crow replied as she observed the man's every movement.

"Where's my brother?" he demanded.

"I don't know where that son of bitch is, last I saw him he was begging for his life," Crow said. She was growing concerned for Coyote.

"Drop the hatchet," the old man ordered as he lunged toward her slowly.

"Tell me where Coyote is and I'll give it all back, all the gold," Crow replied. The fear swelled up inside as she thought about her brother.

The two argued as tension grew. The winds began to howl. The temperature was dropping rapidly and Crow knew if Coyote was in danger, she'd need to act immediately

"Then, we don't have a deal," she spat as she charged toward the man belligerently.

The old man attempted to fire his gun but Crow had him in a trance. Unable to fight back, she launched the hatchet deep into the man's forehead before pulling the blade out gradually. The sound of the ax exiting the man's flesh was primal and satisfying. His body seized and convulsed on the frigid earth below.

~

"This is where the old man said they left him," she muttered to herself in despair.

Crow froze for a moment and surveyed the rugged landscapes, taking note of every sound that radiated in the cold Appalachian air. A faint noise in the distance grabbed her focus as she paid attention to a shadow nestled in the underbrush on the edge of the hillside. Crow maneuvered around forest debris to find her brother buried underneath various limbs and dead tree branches. She called out to him in distress.

"Coyote is that you?"

"Crow..." he replied with the small bit of life he had left in him.

"I hear you, I am coming toward you," she said as she ran over and began pulling the debris off of him. He was trembling and his eyes were closed. His face was cut and battered.

"Coyote, I'm so sorry," she mumbled. "It's going to be tough, but I'm going to carry you down this mountain."

She lifted him, using all her energy to adjust his thin frame up and onto her back. She was grateful he was frail at that moment as she traversed her way down the mountain. The night was icy and bitter. She could feel the ice crystals forming on the ground, crunching with each step she took. Crow could feel her brother's pulse on her back as she carried him further toward level ground.

"Please don't die on me, Coyote. Please," Crow begged. An overwhelming sense of dread was brewing inside of her. She could feel the treacherous bouts of an untold destiny unraveling in her gut. Her instinct unfurled and spewed out of her while she took note of their surroundings. She could feel her brother's spirit slowly seeping out of his body.

Coyote was dying.

CHAPTER THIRTEEN

They made it halfway down the logging road when Coyote started making odd gurgling noises. His body began to seize, then convulse momentarily.

Crow held her brother tightly in her arms. Gutted by fear, she pleaded with her creator, "Spirit, don't take my brother. Please don't take my brother. Coyote, don't die. I can't go on without you. Coyote!" she cried out.

Tears poured down her face. Her heart collapsed within itself. She could feel a blade cut through her soul. Every inch of core filled with grief and sorrow. She fell onto his body and began to weep uncontrollably. "Coyote, I love you so much."

"I love you, too," he mumbled softly as he took his last breath. Coyote drifted off to sleep and his heart stopped beating.

Crow's body felt numb. She sensed a void emerging from inside her belly. She felt defeated and eviscerated.

"I love you so much, Coyote. So much. I'm going to miss you forever. How am I going to go on?" She rested her head gently on his small chest and fell further into bereavement.

Her brother was gone forever and she was all alone in the world. Suddenly, his body began to shapeshift. His skin cracked and his figure started pulsing rapidly. A white light emerged from the center of his body. It morphed into a vibrant ball. It spun swiftly above his corpse before splitting open and erupting a flood of cosmic energy out into the valley below. The orb plummeted back into Coyote's corpse which was transforming and changing shape before Crow. She watched as her brother's human form dissolved and his spirit materialized. The ball of energy pulsated and vibrated rhythmically as his human corpse evaporated and his amulet fell onto the snow. It hit the cold earth and an animal took shape above the gold pendant. It was a coyote. In full amazement, she observed her brother's body in its new form.

"My brother, you weren't kidding," she uttered softly to herself.

The moon hung quietly overhead giving life to the frigid mountain terrain nestled below.

Crow ran her fingers through Coyote's fur and kissed him on the head. She held his left paw in her hand while she sobbed profusely. She kissed him again on the cheek and felt his scruff against her face. Crow placed her hand over where his amputated limb was, but it was now replaced by a beautifully crafted Coyote paw. Tears streamed down her face as she buried herself in his coat. The snow fell harder and harder, accumulating on his dark brown fur. Crow rubbed his snout and cold nose. She gave him one more kiss on his paw before she picked him up and carried him down the mountain.

When she reached the base, she went to the men's carriage and retrieved some firewood, wool, and flint. She began to build a fire, adding the logs from the carriage until it was raging. She picked Coyote's body off the cold earth and laid him over the fire. As the fire burned and singed his fur coat, a horrible smell permeated the air as Crow wept.

"I'm so sorry, Coyote, it's all my fault. All of it. I never meant for any of this to happen," she cried out.

Her soul was gutted. She felt as if a fishing hook had been aggressively shoved into her stomach and then twisted and turned before being torn out of her, taking bits of her spirit and her life with Coyote with each violent motion. Crow shoved her feelings aside for a moment, then reached for a log and threw it onto the flames.

The fire grew in size as Coyote's body prepared for its final transformation. The light of the blaze danced and flickered off the Hemlocks that encased the forest nook she was situated in. A rustle at the edge of the woods line caught her attention.

Crow watched carefully as a creature stepped out from the shadows lurking before her. The being was freakishly large and epic. It stood over forty feet tall as it stood over her patiently. As Crow observed the majestic entity emerging from the darkness, she recognized the creature's face. It was the Nomad. Her eyes grew as she looked up at the gangly, slender figure. Branches and antlers extended from its head as moss, lichen, and forest debris dripped from his crown to his feet. His arms were abnormally long and his fingers were wooden and elongated. His eyes, small and amber, were inviting and peaceful. Tiny lanterns that lingered like sunlight through the tree leaves at dusk. Woven threads of lichen and moss were delicately intertwined and tangled throughout its intricately crafted body.

His presence was dark like a shadow, but his energy was warm and comforting. She recognized that feeling. She'd felt it at different moments throughout their journey and her life. The Nomad had been watching over them both as they traveled through the wilderness. The creature drifted closer to Crow and crouched down before her. He was timid and sheepish. Even hunched over, he loomed above her like a giant old-growth tree. He gazed down at Crow, the tangled debris of dead branches and antlers protruding off his head as he spoke.

"Crow, thank you. I have wandered these mountains for eons alone and abandoned. It was an evil curse, one I wish was not struck upon me. But my time looking over you and Coyote showed me how to love. It is a feeling I will never forget. When I saw that poor baby coyote dying alone after its entire family had been slaughtered by poachers, then I saw your family mourning the loss of your brother, I knew why I came to this Earth. I knew that I had the power to intervene. I am sorry I couldn't save your family, however.

My powers are limited. I have the ability to shapeshift and communicate with other woodland creatures and spirits. I can offer spiritual guidance and allow other souls in transition to shapeshift and take new forms, but I am far from a protector. I am merely a guide. I can invest my energy into piloting one spirit at a time. I did what I could to watch over you both, but I do not control fate or destiny. Unfortunately, my work is done," the Nomad said before he let out a bellowing scream that echoed through the entire Appalachian mountain range.

People everywhere reported hearing the shriek while the creature dissipated into the stars. His organic frame vanished and ascended into the cosmos above Crow. Coyotes began to appear out of thin air and from the shadows of the forest by the hundreds. They howled at the winter moon in unison, the yelping chaotic and unsettling. They continued to holler and howl. The vibration of the yowling shook the trees, causing snow to fall off of them. When they were done serenading the night, they took off in a stampede toward the town below. They went into homes and began dragging the greedy people out of their beds and devouring them. The coyotes ransacked the town and killed all the people who'd succumbed to a life of greed and harming others.

The animals pulled the humans from their beds, from the saloon, and from the streets. They viciously attacked people and ate their bodies alive. Crow could hear the screams from the side of the mountain. Eventually, the noise subsided and Coyote's body turned to ash. Crow was standing there all alone. She felt lost and empty. Her entire family was gone. All because of greed. The image of the Nomad and his words played over and over in her mind and triggered a cascade of memories.

When their mother was pregnant with the twins, she had intense visions and premonitions. She told her husband that she saw a crow and a coyote intertwined in her belly from her mind's eye. The brother and sister were born and given their names; Crow and Coyote. Coyote, however, was born smaller and underdeveloped. A few months later, a harsh winter hit. Coyote became very ill and was dying. Knowing the fate of their baby, the parents decided to offer the infant to the forest spirits.

Both parents ventured deep into the greenwood and left Coyote to transcend peacefully. Their mother watched as he took his last breath before heading back toward the home, leaving the baby to be taken by the woodland creatures dwelling in and beneath the forest canopy. While their mother was singing a song to honor her child, a whimpering infant coyote emerged from the forest. It was covered in blood and badly injured. Knowing the harsh realities, the parents assumed the worst for the pup.

The coyote's parents had been killed by poachers and the pup was slowly dying. Crow and Coyote's mother held the small animal in her hands as the pup, too, passed away. All of a sudden, the parents heard wailing coming from the shadows. They ran into the darkness of the forest and found their infant alive and crying.

Their mother was certain the child had taken its last breath when she left her son in the woods. Their child was alive! They took their baby home and buried the poor coyote pup honorably.

Coyote told Crow when they were children that when he died as a baby, his spirit found the lost pup and the dying animal's soul took over his body. Crow returned to the present where she stood alone in the middle of the vast Appalachian wilderness.

"The Nomad's been watching over us this whole time?" she said out loud.

She thought it over and it made so much sense. Coyote always had an instinctual passion for the legend of the Nomad and it was from his excitement, Crow found her love for the creature and his story. A part of her couldn't help but think that deep down in his soul, Coyote knew the Nomad saved his life.

"What do I do now, Coyote?" she whispered to herself while looking up at the constellations twinkling above.

Just then, a being in a long brown cloak, wearing a fur hood and holding a tall wooden staff, surfaced before her. It lifted its head up and she could see its pale skin and three eyes. It was one of the Moss People.

The being made its way over to Crow. "I am sorry for your loss."

"Thank you," Crow replied, unsure. She noticed the hooded being was a man. He had two big eyes side by side and one smaller third eye centered above the two at his forehead.

"I know how you feel. That family you killed stole my child from me after they ambushed our community one morning. We are nocturnal people and we can not see during the day. They took full advantage of this and attacked our village. They took my son. They killed him and skinned him for his skull and bones, so they could trade them for gold. People around here like to hunt us for our bones as they glow at night. Since we can not see in the daylight, we are easy prey. We have retreated to caves and underground caverns to live and hide out. Come with me, to our cave. You will be safe there. You can get out of this snow and ice," the man said with a tone of sincerity in his voice. His voice was tiny and muffled.

"Alright, let's go," Crow replied, defeated.

She followed the man to an extremely hidden cave entrance where she went into their home. There she was greeted by the entire race of Moss People. They took care of her, fed, and clothed her. They gave her a room and a place where she could be alone.

She'd been there for about a year when one night she went out with them on a night forage. There, they stumbled upon the Nightcap mushrooms.

The Moss People were the only race of humanoids that were not affected by the fungus and its intoxicating state but Crow, however, wasn't. She couldn't help herself and began to consume an entire ring. She felt the mushrooms take over as she entered a psychedelic world of heightened color and complex geometry.

Before she knew it, she was being carried off beneath the forest floor by the Mechanical Elves. They sang and chanted while they carried her deep under the earth. They traveled further and further down below Earth's crust until they reached the underworld.

When Crow awoke, she was at the base of a magnificent Hemlock tree. Its giant evergreen limbs extended as far as the eye could see. There was a beautifully carved black door etched into its trunk. Crow reached out and held the door's gold knob in her grasp as she swung it open, then stepped inside the dense conifer tree. The wooden door slammed shut as crows appeared in the branches of the immense tree. They formed a vast murmuration, then materialized before they disappeared altogether. She gazed around and observed the ancient space.

It was bright and luminous inside.

There, she was greeted by her parents and Coyote. Crow ran over to her family and hugged them firmly, never wanting to let go again.

"Where am I?" she asked.

"Home," Coyote whispered.

Epilogue

Noah closed the tattered book and fastened the clasp on it, taking a deep breath. He paused for a moment. He'd told that story a million times, but now it held more weight than ever before.

"That's the Legend of the Nomad. Now, there's one thing most of you don't know, although some of you who were in my intro class last semester may already know this. For those of you who don't know, this story has been in my family for generations. My great-great-great-great-grandmother on my father's side was Lorna in that story. She told her kids the tale and they told their kids, and so on down the line to me. This is a big reason why I love this story so much, but ultimately what I love most about it is it challenges the way we see the world. If we can prove the validity of the treasure and the skull, then the world of folklore changes as we know it. Are there any questions?" he inquired to the auditorium full of students, who were watching him with undivided attention.

Since his discoveries, the professor and his classes had become the most popular on campus for obvious reasons. A young lady in the front of the class raised her hand.

"Mr. Greene, I have a question," she replied.

"Sure, shoot."

"What I don't understand about the story, is if Crow was carried off to live in the spirit realm as the tale suggests, who would've been around to tell her whole story?" the young woman asked while tapping her pen on her desk in an impatient manner.

"That's a great question. That's only considering the fact that she was whisked away to be with her family, who was on the other side. However, what we know from this tale is that the Mechanical Elves are merely just tricksters and what Crow experiences at the end inside the grand Hemlock tree could be merely a figment of the hallucinogenic mushrooms. Many people reported seeing Crow in the mountains of North Georgia until the early nineteen hundreds. Some folks say they'd see her hunting in the forests. Hatchet, and ax in hand," Noah answered while peering out over his class.

A young male student with a buzzcut raised his hand and spoke. "Why didn't the Nomad guide Crow after Coyote's death, and if he could summon animals to devour humans why didn't he do it sooner or to protect Crow and Coyote's family from being massacred?" he asked with confusion.

"Another great question. As the story suggests, the Nomad can only guide and assist one spirit at a time and only a soul in transition. That wouldn't apply to Crow at the time of Coyote's death. Also, it's believed that since the Nomad was no longer bound by certain constructs that came from guiding

Coyote. He was simply able to release all that energy in a fury after Coyote's death."

Noah glanced across the room at the students filling the lecture hall and continued. "That is all the time we have for today. I'll see you all next week and, hopefully, I'll have more information on Crow's gold. Get your syllabus signed and brought back on Monday. Remember to always keep an eye out for the Nomad when you're in the Appalachian wilderness. The legend says he still lurks in the forests of North Georgia today." Noah nodded at the class as an overwhelming feeling of joy consumed him.

His team searched for years, trying to locate the cave with the real map. Once they did, it took several more years to make sense of it, let alone use it as a tool. The landscapes changed drastically over the years, as well. Eventually, they decided on the general location and spent another two years dialing in the search area. Finally, they managed to find the treasure and rewrite history. They hoped, at least.

A month would go by when Noah's team finally got their final lab results. The gold and chest were authentic and the skull with three eye sockets came back as being human. It was a huge accomplishment for the professor and his squad. Later that spring, Noah got an email from a scuba diver. The email read:

Dear Dr. Greene,

My name is Hudson. I am a professional scuba diver and wildlife photographer for National Geographic. First, I just want to say I am a big fan of your work and have read all the articles that feature your discoveries in the publication. Recently, my team and I were on an expedition off the coast of Ireland. We were doing a deep dive and we encountered some caves that ran far and wide under the ocean. One of my divers noticed this giant petroglyph etched into the cave wall and it matches the drawings found in Georgia, Maine, and Scotland. I have attached a picture of it to this email. It is dark as it's in a cave under the ocean, but this has to be over seven hundred and fifty million years old. We were astonished. My expedition crew and I will be heading back to the spot this summer if you would like to come with us. We're looking at July. Please let me know if you're interested. We'd love to have you and your team there. I look forward to hearing from you.

Regards,

Hudson Reeves

Noah was ecstatic; an underwater depiction of the Nomad would shift their way of thinking about ancient folklore and the history of Earth even more. Validation that the Nomad was wandering the Pangea mountain range before the ocean levels rose, would not only shed light on other primordial myths, legends, and lore, it would also reshape how they viewed creation, myths, and folklore. The professor was more than thrilled, not only was this the oldest known evidence of the legend of the Nomad, but also this one was carved into the wall. The others had merely been painted. It was almost as if the artist knew in the future their work would one day be submerged in the ocean. He looked at the attachment and immediately wrote Hudson back and agreed to join the crew in July.

Summer approached quickly and he was overjoyed by the idea of heading to Ireland to search for the oldest petroglyph on Earth. Noah arrived in Europe on July tenth and the team did their first dive on the twelfth. Noah was nervous but excited. He wasn't too keen on scuba diving and being underwater that long, especially in a cave, but Hudson and his crew assured him he'd be fine. They told him he could easily exit the cave and surface at any time. He spent six months getting his certification and doing deep dives off the coast of Georgia and North Carolina.

The teams descended into the murky, frigid Atlantic waters and to the ancient, ghastly landscapes below. The descent was extensive and it took longer than Noah expected to reach the cave. Anxiety swelled up inside of him while they sunk deeper into the darkness, further below the surface. Everything was bleak and opaque besides the lights coming off of the crew's helmets. They reached the mouth of the cave and Hudson led the way to the hieroglyph. It was a small entrance that quickly opened up into a vast cavern. The team swam further into darkness.

When the expedition squad finally reached the glyph, Noah got the first front-row seat of the primordial artwork. He ran his hands over it and felt its deep grooves and crevices that weaved and etched their way into the ancient mountainside. It was perfectly imprinted into the solid rock wall. The engraving was flawless despite being worn from millions of years of weathering. The light of his helmet filtered over the giant engraving. It was over sixty feet high and the lines were deep grooves scratched far into the hard surface. It was carefully carved and looked as if it had been etched with machinery. The drawing was heavily detailed, yet chaotic. The elongated creature's shape was stretched along the ancient granite. The hieroglyph was monstrous and pronounced as it sat submerged deep beneath the ocean's surface.

While he took in the moment, a scribble at the bottom right corner of the glyph caught Noah's attention. As he peered closer, pressing his mask against the cave wall, he noticed it looked to be a combination of symbols, shapes, and numbers. Eventually, the teams surfaced and climbed onto the boat that undulated in the choppy waves of the Atlantic Ocean.

The professor was perplexed at what could be written on the bottom corner. Noah and his team reviewed the photos and scans they took of the image while the boat made its way back to shore.

"I think we're looking at a signature like an artist would sign their work of art," he suggested, observing the data images coming in on the computer screen.

"None of the other images have signatures, why does this one? The others were also hand painted but this one is carved into the walls of the cave. Why do you think that is?" Hudson asked.

"It's as if the artist knew this would one day be underwater and in an effort to preserve their work, they etched into the rock. They did it with vigor and force. Whoever did this was strong," Noah's assistant replied while the boat zoomed over the ocean waves. The sun peaked out from behind a canvas of clouds and a ray of sun hit Noah's face.

He took a moment to process his thoughts to choose his words carefully before he spoke and said, "The only being at that time with enough strength and determination to carefully construct this ancient work of art while being fully conscious of the future of the planet's evolutionary shift in landscapes and continents, would be the Nomad himself. These images are not a depiction of an artist's experience when greeted by the Nomad. They are simply self-portraits."

"Brilliant!" Hudson exclaimed as he patted Noah on the back.

The expedition was a success and the team retreated to the coast of Ireland, feeling accomplished. When Noah got back to his hotel room in Galway, he pulled out his laptop and turned on the television across from the bed in the room. He took in the moment and relished in the glory. He was rewriting history, bridging the gap between Appalachian and Celtic folklore. He opened his laptop and signed into his email account. He noticed a message from one of his colleagues in the Archaeology department. Noah clicked on the email and began to read the message. His eyes light up as he read the words on the screen.

Hey Noah,

I hope you are enjoying your summer vacation and your time in Ireland. Just wanted to give you a head's up. A young woman named Dawn stopped by your office today. She was looking to speak to you about your work, specifically on the "Legend of the Nomad." She said she is a direct descendant of Crow and she'd like to speak with you. She left me her number and her email address. They are below. Anyway, enjoy the rest of the summer. See you in September!

Noah was taken aback. The pieces began to fall even more into place. He opened a blank email and began putting Dawn's email address in. He wasn't sure what she had to say, however, he couldn't wait to talk with her. He sent her an email and after several back-and-forth messages, they decided to meet in a cafe in Gold City.

"It's so nice to meet you, Dawn," Noah said when they finally met as he smiled and observed her soft features and gentle nature.

"It's nice to meet you, too. I read about your work in the local paper and felt like I needed to reach out. I have pictures. Here," she said as she pulled out a manilla folder and dumped several photographs onto the table.

"Are these of Crow?" Noah asked as he reached for a worn picture and examined it closely.

The pictures were old and vintage. The black and white photographs showed an old woman in fur clothing. She appeared rugged and feral. Her face was serious and her demeanor threatening. In her hand, she was holding a hatchet. Around her neck hung two gold amulets. One of a crow and the other of a coyote.

"Yes, that's Crow. Hold your hand out and close your eyes," she told him with a warm tone.

Noah held both hands out with his palms facing the sky. The breeze brushed against his face as he took in the warmth of the sun on his skin and the bustle of the coffee shop patrons on the cafe patio.

He felt something metal and cool graze against both palms.

"Open your eyes," Dawn told Noah with a smile.

When he opened his eyes, there in both hands sat each amulet. In his right hand, he held a gold crow, and in his left a gold coyote. Noah was astonished and speechless.

"Wow. I don't know what to say." Noah glanced up at Dawn as she gazed at him and spoke.

"That's the real treasure."

Justin Sexton is also a musician and podcaster. He is the creator of the dark fictional podcast series; Project Darkwave with all original music and stories.

QR Code for Project Darkwave:

Book Two of the Cryptid Forest Series coming out Winter 2024!

www.ingramcontent.com/pod-product-compliance
Lightning Source LLC
Chambersburg PA
CBHW030547130626
46552CB00006B/2459